MEET MADAME
Chamberlaine

MEET MADAME Chamberlaine

Tzipie Wolner

MENUCHA PUBLISHERS

Menucha Publishers, Inc.
© 2016 by Tzipie Wolner
Typeset and designed by Rivkah Lewis
All rights reserved

ISBN 978-1-61465-311-0

Published and distributed by:
Menucha Publishers, Inc.
250 44th Street
Brooklyn, NY 11232
Tel/Fax: 718-232-0856
www.menuchapublishers.com
sales@menuchapublishers.com

Printed in Israel

Contents

Acknowledgments

Thank you for the unbelievable support I received from my incredible and warm parents, Mr. Eli and Faigie Reichman; my inspiring and amazing in-laws, Mr. Chaim Efraim and Chana Leah Wolner; my beautiful children, my treasures, and my most remarkable husband, Rabbi Dovid Wolner, my rock.

Thank you to my talented editors at *Mishpacha Junior*: Tzirel Strassman for finding the fun and potential in Madame, Yael Mermelstein for pushing her forward, and Libby Tescher for cementing her into a member of the *Mishpacha*!

Thank you to Menucha Publishers, and to Chaya Silverstone for your detailed and on-target editing.

Thank you to my fan club—you egged me on and on!

Thank You, Hashem. No words would ever be enough.

Meet Madame Chamberlaine

She's coming to New York to visit a friend," my mother explained. "We're all going to treat her with respect. Understood?"

We nodded miserably. She was going to sleep in our room.

Shuly and I were not excited.

Madame Chamberlaine walked in on Tuesday morning. She wore a pink glittery kerchief with swinging tassels. She had huge blue eyes, pink cheeks, and bright red lips. She wore a sweater with tassels all around the hem and a flowing pink skirt. On her feet were pink high heels.

She said, "*Oh, mes petites*," and pecked our cheeks. We grabbed our schoolbags and rushed out.

After school, we opened the front door a crack.

"*Mes petites*," we heard. "Finally you are home. Come in, come in."

We looked at each other. Wasn't it our house? Why was she giving us permission to enter?

The house smelled divine. We ran to the kitchen to see what our mother had baked in honor of our guest.

Madame Chamberlaine was there and gave a tinkling laugh. "*Bon, eh? Goutez une.*" She handed us each a warm pastry with yellow cream inside. *Goutez une* was what they were called? And who was this Madame Chamberlaine that she was offering us one of our mother's baked goods?

My mother sat on a chair and smiled. "Madame Chamberlaine made those. Taste them, they're delicious."

Wow…they were yummy. I had three before I even put my schoolbag down. "These *goutez une*s are great," I told her.

Instead of thanking me for the compliment, Madame's voice rang with laughter until she had tears streaming down her pink cheeks. "*Chèrie*, not these are *goutez une*. *Goutez une* means 'taste one.'"

I smiled. This language stuff was going to be fun, I could tell.

        ⋇ ⋇ ⋇

That evening Madame Chamberlaine cooked supper too, and boy, was it a feast fit for a king. My brothers were hooked on her. They said with food like hers, they wanted her with us forever. As for Shuly and I… Well, Madame wasn't sleeping in their room, was she now?

At bedtime, Madame bid us a "*bon nuit*" and went to sleep. We later tiptoed into our room so as not to wake her. When we were already in bed, I turned to Shuly.

"She's not snoring," I whispered.

"She's not anything like we thought she would be," she whispered back.

Madame turned in her bed. I think I saw her eyes open and give a quick wink.

I closed my eyes and went to sleep.

* * *

Madame Chamberlaine was already in the kitchen when I came down in the morning. I went to get a bowl and spoon for my usual fare of cereal and milk when she stopped me.

"*Non, non, non. Aujourd'hui,* it's pancakes. *Avec* maple syrup." Good stuff. My brothers? They almost didn't want to leave for yeshivah!

All day I was looking forward to coming home to see what Madame was up to. After school, Shuly and I dashed through the door and, sure enough, she was home, with an umbrella in her hand and a green trench coat over her arm.

"*Vite, vite.* Homework and we're off."

"Off? Where are we going?"

"You'll see. *Vite!*"

I finished homework in a jiffy while Madame packed a cardboard box with dainty cream cakes. I watched her wrap the box with pink ribbon.

"*Prête?*" she asked.

"You mean 'pretty'?" I asked as I put my books away.

"*Non, chèrie,* I mean *prête.* It means 'ready.'"

"Oh yes, we are!"

We waved good-bye to my mother and ran after Madame Chamberlaine.

"*Vite, vite, chèries!*" she called.

"Why does she keep calling us cherries?" Shuly giggled.

Madame screeched to a stop. "*Chèrie* does not mean 'cherries.'"

"So what does it mean?" Shuly asked, but Madame was already halfway down the block.

We ran to catch up.

Finally, Madame stopped in front of an imposing red-brick building. She rang the bell.

"Yes?" an old woman asked through the window of the black door.

"I came to see Dora," Madame said.

The door opened and we filed in after Madame. She walked quickly up a narrow staircase and stopped in front of a closed brown door. She rapped twice.

The door squeaked open. A woman with a very thin face stood there. She wore a faded green snood and an old house-coat. Her pale cheeks suddenly turned pink with pleasure and she smiled widely.

"You came back! *Merci*, Madame Chamberlaine."

The two women jabbered in French until Madame gently pushed me toward her friend.

"Be polite. Say hello."

"Hi," I said.

The green-snooded woman smiled meekly. "Will she stay with me?"

"*Oui*, and me too." Madame smiled.

"Oh no, most certainly not, Madame. You have to take care

of yourself," the woman replied.

"Tsk, tsk," Madame said as she placed the pink-ribboned box on a little table. She lowered her voice and asked, "Tell me, how is Jacqueline feeling?"

The thin woman's eyes became sad. "Not too well. Come see." She opened a side door that led to a room with a small bed. A tiny hand stuck out from under the white blanket, and a lot of red hair was draped over the white pillow.

"Who's that?" I whispered.

"That's Jacqueline. The girl was in a terrible car accident, and although there is nothing wrong with her, she still hasn't woken up."

I gasped. "That's terrible. How can I help her?"

"Daven, *chèrie*," Madame said.

I nodded and so did Shuly.

"Also, you can visit her."

"Us? We don't even know who she is. I can't even pronounce her name."

"Doesn't matter. You'll learn."

I looked at Shuly and she pursed her lips and pulled up one eyebrow. I could tell that she wasn't too thrilled with Madame's idea. Believe me, neither was I! Madame Chamberlaine seemed like a fascinating woman with fantastic ideas, but this probably wasn't one of her best.

Shuly and I waited until Madame was through with her visit. We walked home quietly. When we reached our front porch, Madame turned to face us. "*Chèries*, you will visit Jacqueline, *comprendez vous?*"

Whatever that meant, but she'd have to push us to Jacqueline if she wanted us to visit her.

Madame did better. She bribed us. She baked delicious pastries for Shuly and myself after every visit to Jacqueline. We sang to the prone little girl and waited for her to move a bit or say something, but she lay still as a statue. After a few visits, we began feeling really sorry for her; she lay there all day with no visitors aside from ourselves. We asked our friends from school to daven for her and to come too. So they davened and came, and we davened and came, and word spread, and soon so many girls wanted to sing and talk to Jacqueline that we had to make a chart of who could come when. We made a *Tehillim* chart and every girl received one *perek*. So many girls were signed up that we were saying the whole *sefer Tehillim* each week.

Madame Chamberlaine was so glad. She made all sorts of delicacies for the visiting girls and thanked each of them. "It was worth it for me to come from France so that I could introduce you to Jacqueline. *Je suis contente!*"

One day, while Shuly and I were sitting next to Jacqueline, I saw the white blanket move. *Must be the wind*, I thought. But then I recalled that there were no windows in the room, and therefore there couldn't have been a wind.

There it was again! The blanket shook a teeny bit. I slowly walked to the bed and looked at the moving blanket. The tiny fingers were drumming on the blanket. Wait! I turned my eyes to look at the pillow, and hey…staring at me were two of the most beautiful grey eyes I'd ever seen!

"Jacqueline!" I whispered in awe.

She stared at me.

I ran out to get her mother. "Quick, *vite*, come!"

She ran in. Her eyes filled with tears.

It turned out that Jacqueline had heard all our one-sided conversations and all our songs. She said that she didn't understand much of what we said because she speaks mostly French, however, she loved when we sang and spoke to her.

All of us were so happy. Madame was the happiest of us all (well, maybe not happier than Jacqueline's mother). She put her arms around us and said, "So proud of you for arranging the *Tehillim* and visitors, *mes petites.*"

"*Mes petites?*" I asked. Shuly and I looked at each other. "*Chèries, non?*"

Madame Chamberlaine laughed, and so did we.

Fun with FOREIGN WORDS

avec	With
aujourd'hui	Today
bon	Good
bon nuit	Good night
comprendez vous	Do you understand
chèrie(s)	Dear(s)
goutez une	Taste one
je suis contente	I am happy
merci	Thank you
mes petites	My little ones
non	No
oui	Yes
prête	Ready
vite	Fast

What a Day

School was starting the next day and there I was, lying in bed and could not for the life of me fall asleep. I had tried everything: counting sheep, saying *Shema* like thirty times, and even singing myself to sleep with every song I had known since kindergarten.

I went downstairs where my mother and Madame Chamberlaine were chatting. Madame cooked me some warm milk and warned that if I didn't fall asleep I wouldn't be able to wake up early enough to make the bus. Well, you know how it is when someone tells you something like that—I became doubly worried and of course couldn't fall asleep!

In my room, I kept hearing my alarm clock ticking, and every now and then I peeked out from under my covers to look at the time. It was getting later and later and…yikes, even later!

I don't know how I finally fell asleep, but I do know that waking up was a disaster. I heard screaming and I opened my eyes to see Shuly all dressed in her school uniform, her hair brushed into a side ponytail, shrieking something or other.

"What? Be quiet and lemme go back to sleep," I mumbled.

Then it hit me that it was the first day of school!

I jumped and grabbed the alarm clock. "Shuly, why didn't you wake me? The bus will be here in five minutes."

"Four," Shuly said as she ran to get her stuff.

I can't remember ever getting ready so fast. Good thing I'd prepared my schoolbag the night before, otherwise I would have been a royal mess. In four minutes flat, I was flying out the door to catch up to Shuly. My mother shoved two cookies into my hands as I raced past her—and boy, did I run.

I saw the bus rounding the corner. I ran, my schoolbag sliding off my shoulders as it kept hitting my back with every stride. Run, run, run! I nearly reached the corner when I tripped and fell facedown on the sidewalk. The bus was going to pull away without me, so I picked myself off the ground and hobbled over to the open door of the bus. Shuly helped me on and as I passed the other girls on the bus, they were all staring at me.

"What's the matter with me? Why are they all looking at me like that?" I whispered to Shuly.

"Uh…you…uh…look dirty."

"Why thanks."

What a way to start the year.

I huddled into my seat and turned my face to the window. Yes, if you must know, I was crying. Nothing major. No rainstorms, just a slight drizzle that made my face damp and maybe would rinse off some of the grime that had settled on my nose when I fell. All my friends, who I hadn't seen all summer, were on the bus, talking and laughing, and I was cowering in my seat, davening so hard that they wouldn't find me and my red, puffy eyes.

When the bus stopped, I waited until all the girls went off. I made a detour to the bathroom to check out my status in the mirror and in privacy.

Wow. I touched my nose to make sure it was really mine. Come to think of it, it did feel kind of funny. It was bright red and had black gook all over it. My nose was not all that large, but there was a whole lot of dirt hugging it! There was a scratch on my left cheek. Everything else looked fine.

I bent down to check my knees. Ouch. Two big scrapes on each knee and two big holes in my tights to see them. (By the way, those were new tights I was wearing.) The blood was already drying up. Ewww.

I washed my knees with wet paper towels (it hurt!) and splashed water on my face (it felt refreshing) and put my bag on my back. We hadn't even started school yet and I was ready to go home.

When I swung the bathroom door open, the halls were quiet. Too quiet. This couldn't be happening—I was going to be late on the first day? No way.

I walked fast to my new classroom. I didn't want to run because I knew how my principal hated when we did, and that was one person I did not want to meet on my first day. Phew, my classmates were all sitting in their seats, but no teacher was yet in sight.

I still needed to find a seat before my teacher came. That wasn't too hard. All the seats were taken besides one—right next to the window. Good, I liked the window seat even if it got cold in the winter. I hung my schoolbag on my chair and waited.

Morah Jacobs walked in. We all stood up and looked at one another. She was a new teacher and none of us knew whether she would be nice or not. She was not smiling and looked stern. A bit scary, even.

She asked us to sit and to each to say our names. I was beginning to relax and think that maybe the day wouldn't turn out to be so awful when Morah Jacobs told us to take out a new notebook and a pencil. That I knew I had.

I turned to get my schoolbag and wanted to unzip it when I saw that the zipper was already open. Huh? I peered in. No, no, no… My schoolbag was empty!

How did I not realize that I was carrying around an empty bag? And where did all my new stuff go? That time it *was* a rainstorm that hit my face. I bawled so loud that Morah Jacobs came to see what had happened. How was I supposed to tell her that I'd bought the Hello Kitty pencil case last year in some random store in Manhattan and my eraser was the cutest from my cousin's eraser collection and…and…and…I hiccupped and cried and Morah Jacobs told me to go wash my face in the bathroom.

It was so embarrassing.

I sniffled and sat up straight at my desk. I thought I saw pink tassels shaking in the wind somewhere outside. I stared out the window. Definitely something pink. And hey, pink shoes!

Morah Jacobs was looking at me a little strangely. "Do you want to go wash up or are you okay?"

Was I smiling? Because I felt like smiling.

"Yes, I want to go wash up." I ran out and bumped right into the pink tassels. "Madame! How did you know that I needed you?" I hugged her.

"Ah, *ma petite*. I just did."

She laughed, which made me feel that everything would be all right. She handed me a shopping bag.

"*Çela appartient a toi?*"

"Madame! Where did you find it?"

"When you ran to catch your *autobus*, I saw stuff flying out of your *cartable*. By the time I came out to get it, you were long on the *autobus*."

She saw my wet face.

"*Viens, chèrie*, let me help you wash up."

She helped me do that and also cleaned my knees. She took two Band-Aids out of her pocket. Then she laughed.

"Oops, I almost forgot." She opened her purse and took out a package of new tights. "*Pour toi*." She smiled.

"How did you know I tore mine?"

She laughed. "I just did. Now you can start your day again, fresh and clean, and you have all your school supplies."

I smiled. "Maybe you can do something about Morah Jacobs so she'll be nice to me?"

"Nonsense, I'm sure she's a teacher that is *merveilleuse*! You be kind to her and she'll be kind to you."

Madame walked me back to my classroom. "You'll be okay now?" she asked.

Before I could answer, the door opened and there stood Morah Jacobs. "I was wondering what was taking you so long."

Then she looked at Madame Chamberlaine, and before I knew it they were hugging and jabbering in—you guessed it—French!

Like Madame would say, *oh là là*!

I slipped into the classroom and thought that if Morah Jacobs was a friend of Madame Chamberlaine, she probably was a teacher that was *merveilleuse*!

Fun with FOREIGN WORDS

autobus	Bus
cartable	Schoolbag
çela appartient a toi	Does this belong to you
merveilleuse	Marvelous
pour toi	For you
viens	Come
DO YOU REMEMBER THIS ONE?	
ma petite	My little one

The Sweet Surprise

I pressed my nose to the living room window. Where was she already?

Shuly tapped her foot. "Do you think she missed her flight?"

"I certainly hope not."

"Look, I see pink and frills. It must be her!" I yelled as I yanked the front door open and raced down the steps.

I ran right into Madame Chamberlaine's large pink bag.

"*Ah, ma petite!*" She hugged me.

"We thought you weren't coming," Shuly said.

"*Moi?* I said I would come, *non?*"

"Oh, Madame," my mother said when we reached our porch.

"You must be so tired. Rest before Rosh HaShanah comes in."

"Rest? *Bien non.* I have somewhere special to go before *yom tov.*"

Shuly and I began to jump. "Can we come with you?"

She smiled as she took out plain white boxes from her bag. The aroma coming from them was absolutely delicious.

"Honey chocolate chip cookies for *mes petites,*" she said with a wink.

We waited patiently while Madame washed up and drank. Then we were out and in a taxi before we remembered that we didn't even know where we were going.

We traveled and rode and got a tiny bit bored when Madame Chamberlaine lay her head back on the headrest and closed her eyes. She must have been tired from her long flight from France. Finally, the taxi stopped. Madame's eyes popped open and she smiled.

"*Très bien.*"

She paid the driver and we climbed out. I looked around. All I saw were trees and flowers. Birds were chirping and bees were humming. Very pretty indeed, but why did Madame bring us to such a place a few hours before Rosh HaShanah?

Suddenly, I noticed a man dressed all in white, with huge white rubber gloves that reached past his elbows. He held a large white hat that looked like a cross between a motorcycle helmet and a Purim mask.

"He looks like he belongs in a spaceship," I whispered to Shuly.

"This is my cousin, Yudel," Madame explained. "He is not an astronaut, by the way. He is a beekeeper."

"Eww," Shuly said. "Does that mean we're going to come

home with bee bites? I don't like them."

"No sudden movements, girls, and you'll be fine," Yudel piped up.

"We're getting fresh honey for Rosh HaShanah. Come see what Yudel will do."

Madame led us to a white cupboard that I didn't notice before. Who needed a cupboard in the middle of the forest?

Yudel slipped his hat on and we watched as he picked up a little metal container with a spout that had smoke coming out.

Shuly and I backed off. What was going on? If Yudel wanted to start a fire so close to the trees, that was his problem, but I didn't want to be involved.

Madame laughed. "*Viens, mes chéries.* The bees don't like the smoke either. This pushes them deep into the hive so they don't bother us."

I saw a bee buzzing over my head and I ducked. I wasn't sure I liked this outing very much. Too much flying stuff and too scary with all the bees so close in that cupboard. I looked at Shuly. She didn't look too happy either.

Yudel removed the top of the cupboard and then lifted a rectangular shelf from inside. It was brown with lots of white stuff, almost like the wax of a candle. Despite my fear, I inched a bit closer. What *was* that?

Yudel shook the frame and lots of furry bees fell off. I backed away fast. It was so gross. He put the shelf to the side and repeated the same thing with about five other frames.

By the time Yudel was up to his sixth, Shuly and I were far, far away from him. We had asked to come with Madame, but had we known we were going to visit bees we would've stayed safe and snuggly in our home eating yummy honey cookies!

"Madame," I yelled. "We have honey in our house. We don't need more."

We backed further away and then heard Madame calling, "Stop! *Arrêtez!*"

Did she expect us to go back to the bees?

I bumped into something hard and fell. I looked back and shrieked, "Ahhhh! Another hive!"

Shuly stood in shock as angry bees started flying out of the hive and buzzed all around us.

"I don't want to be stung!" I shrieked.

"Me neither," Shuly sniffled.

We didn't know: Should we get up and run or stay put?

"Yudel said that if we're still they won't bite," Shuly recalled.

We looked on, our eyes round. I saw circling bees reflected in Shuly's enlarged pupils.

"Does it say anywhere in '*Unsaneh Tokef*' about dying through bee bites?" I asked Shuly as I lay curled up on the floor.

My sister shrugged. "I don't know, and I'm not sure I want to find out."

A bee landed on my wrist. I wanted to shake him off and yell, but heard Madame saying, "Keep still, *chèrie*, and it won't sting."

The tiny legs moved up my arm. They tickled me and felt horrible. I began to cry softly. I didn't want the bees on me; I didn't want to be there at all.

I saw pink. Madame! She held the smoker in her hand and sprayed us with smoke. The bee flew off my arm. The swarm of bees that had surrounded us flew into their hive.

"Thank you, Madame!"

"Why did you run off, *mes petites*?"

"We were scared."

"Come, come. They don't touch you if you don't bother them. Let's go with Yudel to extract the honey from the frames."

"Will there be bees?"

Madame laughed. "*Non*, just us and the honey."

We followed Madame to a little hut. Yudel was already inside. He was holding a bee frame in one hand and a steaming knife in the other, and he was scraping the white stuff off the frame.

"I'm removing the wax from the honey," he explained. When he finished scraping one frame, he placed it into a huge plastic container with a spout at the bottom. Then he did the same with the next frame. He completed all the frames and placed them into the plastic container. He closed the lid and asked, "Who will be the first to turn this handle?"

Since there were no bees, I offered. I turned slowly at first and then Yudel said, "Faster, faster. Turn as fast as you can."

I did and was sweating soon enough. Shuly took over, then Madame finished off. Yudel opened the cover, peeked in, and said, "Yup! The honey is all extracted. Let's put it into bottles."

He took an empty plastic bottle off a shelf and placed it under the spout. He opened the spout and out came sticky brown honey!

"Wow, so awesome."

"*Oui, eh?*" Madame winked. "I thought you would enjoy it."

Yudel filled up two bottles for us and the rest he kept for himself to give to his family and friends. He took us back to our house. We had just enough time for a shower and a quick nap before *yom tov*.

After shul, we walked home and wished everyone a *shanah*

tovah. When my father dipped the challah in the honey, his eyes lit up. "With honey like this, we're sure to have a sweet new year."

When it was my turn to taste the challah with the honey, I saw that my father was totally right. The honey was sweeter and tasted better than any honey I'd ever tasted. Maybe those bees weren't so bad after all.

Madame winked at me over the table, as though she knew what I was thinking. "*Une bonne et douce annèe!*" she said with a smile.

"And a sweet year to you, Madame!"

Fun with FOREIGN WORDS

arrêtez	Stop
bien non	Why, no
mes chèries	My dears
moi	Me
très bien	Very good
une bonne et douce annèe	A happy and sweet year

DO YOU REMEMBER THESE?

non	No
mes petites	My little ones
oui	Yes
viens	Come

Up to Our Necks with Babies

I came home from school one day and stopped.

Huh?

On the front door was a little sign with a baby on it and it said, "Babies on Board." Did my mother have a baby—I mean, babies?

I opened the door and heard the crying of a newborn.

"Hello? Is this my house?"

"Shhh." My mother stuck her head out of the kitchen. "I'm trying to put the baby to sleep."

I came into the kitchen, where my mother was rocking a baby on her shoulder.

"Whose baby is that?" I whispered.

She put a finger to her lips and mouthed, "Soon."

I grabbed a pear from the fridge and a banana from the counter and sat down. As I was biting into the banana, I heard a baby cry. The baby on my mother's shoulder was finally asleep. Oh no, don't tell me that babies cry in their sleep too! But the sound was coming from somewhere outside the kitchen. This I needed to see.

I went to investigate. On the rug in the living room was another baby, bawling her poor eyes out. There was a pacifier next to her, so I stuck it into her little mouth. She quieted down, pulled the blanket closer, and fell asleep.

You're going to think I'm making this up, but then I heard another baby crying! I ran to the kitchen to see if the baby on my mother's shoulder had woken up. Not only was that baby sleeping, but my mother's eyes were closed too. I never knew that people could sleep standing up; I thought only horses do that. But then again, mothers can do anything, right?

Okay, so the baby on my (sleeping) mother's shoulder was asleep, and so was the baby in the living room. Where else do adults keep babies?

I followed the crying and ended up in my father's study. A baby was lying in our old infant seat, his tiny fists flying and poking the air around him. Wow, somebody looked mad.

No pacifier. No bottle either. I rocked him gently, but he refused to keep quiet.

"Fine, little buster, I'll hold you."

I held him and then, wonder of wonders...I heard another baby crying! I peeked into the living room. The baby there was still asleep and so was the pair in the kitchen. I was holding a quiet baby. That made *three* quiet babies, yet a child somewhere was hollering. Don't tell me there was *another* baby in the house!

Folks, I was not imagining things, though I had to pinch myself to make sure but…yikes. I found another one! It was turning into an exciting game of "Let's See How Many Crying Babies We Can Fit under One Roof."

The fourth baby was howling like a kitten, curled up in our stroller. Holding one little guy against my shoulder, I rocked the stroller back and forth until the baby inside quieted down. Then I felt my shirt get all wet.

It. Was. Not. Funny.

I don't know if the baby had a dirty diaper or if he was spitting all over me, but it was gross. I put the baby back in the infant seat, then the baby in the stroller began to cry, then the baby in the living room had a mighty cow, and before I could even blink there was a fine crying choir being orchestrated right under my nose.

Oh boy.

I didn't know whose babies they were, but could the mother please come and take them back?

I heard my mother calling something from the kitchen. I went in to see what she wanted.

"Good, you heard me over this racket. Darling, I'm exhausted. I offered to care for Mrs. Pink's quadruplets for the day. Her hired help needed a week off and frankly, I don't blame her. I took care of these babies for one morning and I think I need a month off. Do you mind if I take a quick nap and you care for these cuties with Shuly?"

Did she just call these babies cuties? All four of them were red in the face and competing who could cry the loudest, and she called them cuties?

Shuly walked through the door as my mother disappeared.

"Shuly, I hope you like babies more than I do."

"I thought you loved babies," my sister replied.

"Well, I used to. Not anymore. Well, not these anyway. Well, I do like these, but I honestly don't appreciate four screaming 'cuties' at once."

"Okay, so you'll take care of two and I'll do two. We have two hands for a reason, huh?"

I took the two that were screaming less loudly, but as soon as I held them, I felt my ears going numb.

"How're you managing, Shul?" I yelled over the noise. "Still love babies?"

She made a face.

I ran with the two babies to the playroom and took out a paper and thick marker. I made a huge square and wrote, "Beware of Babies!" Then under that I wrote, "Do not enter! They are louder than you!"

Shuly laughed as I hung it on the front door. And the babies continued yelling their little lungs out.

I began to feel sorry for them, but whatever Shuly and I tried just didn't work. They refused to calm down.

"I give up!" I yelled. "Any fresh ideas would be nice."

Shuly held her baby-filled hands up. "Sorry, sis. I'm frazzled and clueless like you."

Then the doorbell rang. Who would enter such dangerous territory was anyone's guess. But I was sure happy to use an extra pair of hands, especially some more experienced ones.

Boy, was I glad to see who was at the door: Madame Chamberlaine!

"How did you know to come?" I asked as I thrust the babies into her arms.

"*Oh là là! Mes petites*, what's going on here?" Her pink cheeks became bright red like tomatoes and she squealed, "*Des bèbès!*"

She held a baby on the crook of each elbow and cooed. "*Mes pauvre petits bèbès!* Cootcha, cootcha!"

The babies in Shuly's arms suddenly became quiet too and listened to Madame "cootchy-cootchying" in French. Wow, I could finally hear myself think.

"Uh, Madame, you think you can stay to care for these… cuties?" I asked.

"*Oui, ma petite!* What a pleasure. What a treat."

She sat on the couch, four babies on her lap, and she cooed and laughed and soothed and played until one by one each baby closed his or her eyes and slept. Madame covered them gently and tiptoed out of the living room.

"*Maintenant, mes filles deserve un petit peu attention*," she said with a laugh. "Both of you look like you have just gone through a car wash without a car."

In fifteen minutes the house smelled delicious. Madame baked one of her yummy cakes; as soon as she was done we heard squealing coming from the living room.

Shuly and I looked at each other. "Uh-oh."

Madame smiled. "*Très bien! Les bèbès* are up." She ran to calm them.

My mother appeared in the kitchen. She held a small paper that said "Do Not Disturb" in her hand. "Who hung this on my doorknob?"

Madame came back to the kitchen with two babies. "*Ah, ma chèrie*. I did. I didn't want anyone to wake you."

My mother laughed. "I sure slept well. But I see that everything is under control. Thank you, Madame!"

The doorbell rang. I opened the door and saw my next-door neighbor standing outside with a baby in her arm.

"Mrs. Pink told me that there's a good babysitter in your house. Do you mind if I leave my baby with you for a few minutes?"

I didn't know what to say, so she put the baby in my hands and left.

As I was closing the door I saw three more neighbors marching toward our house with babies in their arms. Oh no. This was not happening. I quickly closed the door, but then heard Madame's heels right behind me.

"More babies? What fun! Tell them all to come." She opened the door. I opened my eyes wide when she said, "And you will help me."

She tore off the sign I had posted on the front door earlier and replaced it with, "Bunch of Babies—Please Enter. They Are Loads of Fun!"

And you know what? We had a ton of fun. (But between you and me, don't ask me to babysit for the next couple of months…)

Fun with FOREIGN WORDS

des/les bèbès	The babies
maintenant	Now
mes filles	My girls
mes pauvre	My poor
petits bèbès	Little babies
un petit peu	A little bit

DO YOU REMEMBER THESE?

chèrie	Dear
mes petites	My little ones
oui	Yes
très bien	Very good

The Gorgeous Birthday Gift

ham! Akiva banged the door. "Hey, Shprintzi! Come quick!"

I took the steps two at a time.

"There's a parcel for you!"

"Me?" I'd never received a package before. "Who's it from?"

"Dunno. Ask the mailman."

I took the small brown envelope and turned it over. All it said was my name and address. While my mother signed for the parcel, I ran to the couch and ripped the paper.

A tiny gold bag fell to the floor. Carefully, I opened it and gasped. Inside was the most exquisite pair of earrings I'd ever seen. They were gorgeous, colorful crystal beads hanging from a heart.

"Those are lovely," my mother said as she came close. The sun that came in through the open door caught the crystal's shine, and it looked as though the beads were dancing.

"And I don't even know who sent them," I said.

"Wait, look. There's a paper on the floor." I bent to pick it up.

> To my chèrie,
> Bon anniversaire to you!
> So, ma petite, do you know what to give a 900-pound gorilla on his birthday?
> I don't know either, but you better hope that he likes it!
> I'm giving you these pretty boucle d'oreilles, and I know that you'll love them. I made them myself and hope you enjoy them as much as I enjoyed making them for you.
> With lots of my love,
>
> Madame Chamberlaine
>
> France

"Wow! She remembered. My birthday isn't until next Tuesday. She's early."

I slipped off my red studs and replaced them with the magnificent pair. I looked like a princess (if I may say so myself)! They glistened and twinkled, and I didn't know much about gorillas, but I absolutely loooved them!

I wore the new earrings for the rest of the day. Before I went to sleep, I carefully lay them on my dresser (y'know, so they'd be the first thing I'd see the following morning).

I woke up early, and after washing *negel vasser* I stretched out my hand for my treasure from France. The beads felt cool, fine, and refreshing. I brought them to my face so that I could admire them that much better and—

"Ahhhhhhhh!"

My father ran into my room, his eyes half-closed, my mother following close behind. Then my brothers screeched in one after the other. Shuly stared from her bed.

"My earring! I have only one earring!"

"Can't be," said my mother. "Weren't you wearing two last night?"

I nodded, feeling the tears prickling the corners of my eyes. "I put both on my dresser last night. Now there's only one!"

"Oh no," my mother said. Then she looked at her watch. "It's not even five in the morning. Go back to sleep, Shprintzi. We'll find it later, when I can open my eyes all the way."

I watched the whole troop waddle out of my room and felt worried. I couldn't wait another two hours!

I lay back down in my bed. I heard Shuly breathing softly. I closed my eyes but couldn't sleep. What if a robber had crept into our house in the middle of the night and stole the earring? *Silly*, I told myself, *where would he come in from?* The window appeared locked. Maybe one of my brothers was playing a joke on me and took one. But that couldn't be either; they all looked so concerned when they came in before, and besides, they all loved Madame Chamberlaine. They wouldn't do anything she wouldn't approve of.

I couldn't sleep. I saw the sun trying to peek into my bedroom through the thick pink curtains. I threw the covers off and crept out of bed. Only one earring shone on the dresser.

I lifted all the papers and books that were lying there too. Nothing. It was as though the earring had disappeared into the air. I heard soft knocking on the bedroom door. Akiva poked his head in. He was all dressed.

"I almost need to leave for davening," he whispered. "Want me to help you look for your earring before I go?"

"Please!"

He walked to the dresser and slid his fingers all over the smooth wood. Then he dropped to his knees and combed his fingers through the carpet. I crouched beside him and did the same. We found nothing.

He stood up. "I need to leave. I'll help you look for it later, 'kay?"

As he walked away, I saw something shiny under his shoe.

"Hey!"

I lunged and dove to the floor. It was the earring, but…it…was…all…smashed…up!

"No, no…"

Akiva saw it. "Oh… This must be so upsetting for you. Maybe I can help you fix it later."

I didn't even say good-bye to him. How could I? He was for sure the one who smashed up the earring. He was the only one wearing shoes that morning. The earring probably fell from the dresser and…oh, oh, oh! I was not upset; I was devastated.

I picked up the ruined earring and cuddled it in my hand. I tried to stop the tears from falling, but after a few swipes, I gave up. I hadn't even worn the earrings for a full day.

I got ready for school and when I came down, my mother said, "Did you find the earring? I was thinking that maybe you should check on the carpet. It probably fell."

Duh.

"I found it already."

"*Baruch Hashem!* So you decided to wear them only on Shabbos?"

I shook my head. "The earring is smashed."

"What? Who smashed it?"

She asked, didn't she? I was about to tell her that Akiva did. Then I thought, Akiva came to help me. He didn't mean to smash it up. How could I blame him?

I shrugged.

My mother came to hug me. "Oh, sweetie, that must be so hard."

Of course the tears came in buckets.

I told myself that I would not be mean and I would not tell anyone that it was Akiva who stepped on my earring. Oh boy, it was hard, especially when he fought with me later that day, but I kept quiet even if I was burning mad.

I looked at my beautiful earring before I went to sleep that night. I could never get another one like it. Madame had written that she made them specially for me.

"Did you write a thank-you note to Madame?" my mother asked as she covered me with my blanket.

"Uh…do I have to? I'm not exactly wearing them."

"She made them for you. I'm sure she worked really hard."

I sighed. So much aggravation from one pair of earrings. I wrote the letter the next day and mailed it. Let me assure you that I did it without a smile.

The day of my birthday arrived and I allowed myself to smile a bit. I was a year older, after all. My mother surprised me with a yummy, three-layered, mocha-vanilla birthday cake, and I was feeling quite happy. After we all sang and ate and everyone in the family gave me *berachos*, my mother handed me a small box.

"This came for you today."

Carefully, I opened it. I gasped. Inside was one beautiful earring. A replacement for the smashed-up one. There was a folded paper inside too.

> *Chère Shprintzi,*
>> *Bon anniversaire for real this time!*
>> *I made you another earring because I heard what happened to the other one.*
>>> *Madame Chamberlaine*
>>> *France*
>
> *PS You have a caring brother. Be thankful.*

I looked up and caught Akiva's eyes. He winked.

"You told her?" I asked him.

"For me to know and for you not to find out!" He laughed. "I'm sorry I stepped on the earring, and thanks for not blaming me."

"*Bien sûr.*"

And the earrings? They look marvelous, and by the way, I now keep them in a special box. The dresser doesn't work that well.

Fun with FOREIGN WORDS

bien sûr	Certainly
bon anniversaire	Happy birthday
boucle d'oreilles	Earrings

DO YOU REMEMBER THESE?

chèrie	Dear
ma petite	My little one

The Tissue Paper Mummy

Madame Chamberlaine was visiting again, but instead of enjoying her company, I jumped every time someone spoke too loud. I shivered every time I heard whispers and freaked out every time I heard a window slam. You see, over the past three weeks there had been seven robberies on our street! Creepy, isn't it? So don't blame me for feeling nervous and scared.

Well, Madame would have none of that.

"*Quoi?* You will not live because maybe a robber will come?" She shook her head, her long pink tassels gently tapping my cheeks.

I nodded. That was pretty much the gist of it, in case she didn't realize. I wasn't scared; I was petrified! What would I do if a thief came into my house while everyone was asleep? What would I do if I was the only one home and he came? What would you do? What would Madame Chamberlaine do?

I needed to ask her.

She laughed. "*Chèrie*, I will worry about it when it happens."

"Really, Madame," I begged. "You laugh, but I don't think it's funny."

"Oh, *ma petite*! Me neither. I just daven that Hashem shouldn't send me any robbers. And if He does, then I daven that He should help me."

That didn't help me very much. Because, boy, was I davening that no thieves come to my house—but we don't always know what's best for us. So I sat on the couch, chewing my nails off and cowering at the tiniest creak coming from the basement. Madame kept nudging me to do this and that and the other thing, but I couldn't move away from my nails.

Well, she decided that she'd had enough of my nonsense, so she came into the den with a big box.

"*Viens, chèrie! On va s'amuser maintenant!*"

She clapped her hands and since I didn't understand her, I stayed in my little corner on the couch.

"Fun!" she said.

Fun when I felt so rotten and scared? I think not.

Madame thought otherwise. She dragged me to the center of the rug and opened the box. She invited Shuly (who wasn't even concerned about the robbers) and my brothers (who couldn't wait for the thieves to come so they could try all their karate chops and kicks on them). We gathered around and watched Madame take out masking tape, which she used to tie our feet together; then we had to race across the hallway.

When she had us in hysterical laughter, she took out straws and string and before long, I couldn't even remember what I was so worried about before because I was so busy giggling!

When the box was almost empty and we'd laughed so much that we weren't sure what was even so funny anymore, Madame reached into the bottom of the carton and pulled out rolls of tissue paper.

We all burst into giggles.

"Madame, for real? Tissue paper?"

She laughed. "*Bien oui!* This is the best part!"

"Okay. We're ready," my brothers said.

"Us too," Shuly and I chimed in.

"Good. We'll do brothers versus sisters."

I rubbed my hands. "Girls rule! Girls rule!"

My brothers chanted louder, "That's what you think! That's what you think!"

Madame gave us a stern look that we had never seen before and we quickly became silent.

"Okay, the game goes like this: One of you will hold the roll of tissue paper and cover the person in your team completely. Roll it around her or him until only the eyes are visible. Whoever finishes first is the winner. Ready, set, go!"

The race began. Shuly rolled the tissue paper around me starting from the top of my head. Soon, my arms were pinned to my sides and my feet were glued together. Yet the tissue paper continued to cover me.

"Ma…er! Ma…er!" I yelled. I meant to yell, "Faster! Faster!" Shuly, of course, couldn't understand because my mouth was all covered. And in case you didn't know, tissue paper and a wet mouth are not a good match. "Ew" is more like it.

Shuly was almost done. The roll was emptying and was unraveling quicker and quicker. Then, bingo! The end flailed in the air and we won!

My brothers could not accept defeat. They came running in my direction, and with my feet stuck together, I tried to get away from them. However, I couldn't. I jumped away (quite literally) and leaped out of the den, with my brothers close behind. I made a sharp jump onto the basement steps and jumped down the stairs before they realized where I had gone. I reached the bottom and leaped into the playroom… and froze. Standing by the window, his dark hand opening the latch to our window…was a robber!

I couldn't move. What did Madame say she would do if a robber came into her home? She said that she would worry about it then. Well, then became now and now I couldn't think. I stood there and the thief noticed me. He stared, shrieked, and ran away so fast that I wasn't sure if it was a dream (you know I mean nightmare) or not. I heard my brothers racing down the steps. I was never happier to see them.

They looked at me and of course saw only my eyes, but my eyes must have looked weird because they said, "What's the matter?"

I ripped the tissue paper from my mouth and began to sob. "There…there…was a robber by the window!"

They saw the open window.

"So where is he now?"

I giggled in the middle of my tears. "I think I scared him."

They looked at me and burst out laughing.

"Come to think of it, you do look a bit like a mummy

in all that tissue paper. You probably scared the thief out of our neighborhood."

Madame Chamberlaine was right beside me. She draped her long hand over my shoulders and said, "You see, Hashem always helps."

My brothers teased me for the next couple of months about me being a tissue paper mummy. But I didn't care because I had the last laugh. I did scare the robber out of our neighborhood; nobody on our street had another break-in!

Fun with FOREIGN WORDS

bien oui	Of course
on va s'amuser maintenant	We will have some fun now
quoi	What
DO YOU REMEMBER THESE?	
chèrie	Dear
ma petite	My little one
viens	Come

The Disappearing Cat

The snow was fluttering down and covering the dirty grey sidewalks. I wished Madame Chamberlaine was around to enjoy the snow with us. She said that she loved the winter. And I? Well, I liked every season as long as Madame was right there with me to enjoy it.

Things had been boring lately. It was school, school, and, oh yes, did I mention it—school. I liked my teachers and all, but I needed a shake-up, some excitement, some tra-la-la to put some spunk into the school days. In short: I needed Madame Chamberlaine.

I was turning the corner to my street when I saw something weird. The snow was sticking to the ground, but one small spot on the sidewalk remained grey and dreary. I came nearer and saw that lying on the floor was a wallet. It seemed that Hashem wanted me to find it because the snow was not covering it up.

I picked it up and looked ahead. All I saw was falling snow and a hazy sky. I looked behind me. Quite deserted there too.

I held the cold, wet wallet in my gloved fingers and felt the dampness coming through my mittens. I ran home and nearly shrieked for joy. There was Madame Chamberlaine with tassels hanging from her *tichel* and pink frilly skirt, looking up at the sky and letting the snowflakes fall on her pink cheeks.

"Madame, you're back!" I hugged her fiercely and she tickled me under the chin.

"*Chèrie!* How have you been?"

"I missed you!"

"Me too. Shall we go inside the house so that I can make you a nice *chocolat chaud*?"

"Yum. Please!"

I dropped the wallet on the floor while I undid my boots and wet, sticky, cold wrappings. Madame picked it up.

"What's this?"

"I found it outside."

Madame smiled. "Ah, you will do *hashavas aveidah*?"

"Well, as soon as I drink your hot chocolate I will."

Shuly and my mother joined us at the table, and while we sipped I opened the wallet. There was a name on a piece of paper, but it was wet and the ink had smudged.

The paper was passed around but no one could read it. Madame held it close to her nose and said, "P-o-d-h… Hmm, I can't seem to read the rest."

Stuck.

She snapped her fingers.

"*Oui*, bring me a phone book, *s'il vous plait*, and we'll find the name. How many names begin with p-o-d-h?"

We flipped through the telephone book and reached the letter *P*.

Bingo! We found it instantly: Podhertzer.

Madame was beaming, my mother was smiling, Shuly and I looked at each other.

"Uh, did you notice that there are three Podhertzers?"

Madame laughed. "*Trois?* That's nothing. We'll call them all."

She called the first one on the list. A man answered and didn't understand what she wanted. At the second try, a woman answered with a shaky voice.

"Talk louder!" she yelled. Shuly and I giggled when Madame held the phone away from her ear.

"*Bien sûr!*" Madame shouted. "Did you lose a wallet?"

"*G-t in himmel*, I sure did. I don't know vat I vill do! All my money, all my papers. Vat vill be?"

"Tsk, tsk," Madame said. "Not to worry, Madame Podhertzer, we will bring it to you. Just give me your address."

We heard yelling coming from the telephone. Madame held the phone far from her ear again and rubbed her ear. "Never mind," she said when the old woman stopped yelling. "I'll find your address where I found your telephone number. See you." She quickly hung up. "*Alors, mes chères*, who's coming with me?"

She didn't have to ask twice. We were in our coats in a jiffy.

Madame danced out. "Ah, *neige*! Nothing like it."

Shuly whispered, "Does *neige* mean 'snow'? I think I like

the English word better. *Neige* sounds like she she's talking about my nose in a different language."

We laughed.

The house Madame was looking for was a block away. It was a wreck, but looked quite pretty in the snow. There was…I don't know what…lots of *stuff* in the front garden. The snow did a good job covering it. I hoped there weren't lions and snakes hiding there. But there couldn't have been, otherwise the mounds of snow would have been walking around.

The door had no color—how weird is that? It looked like there was paint there at some point, but it was either scratched or peeled off over the years. Madame knocked because of course the bell wasn't working.

A lady, who must have been one hundred years old, opened the door. She had a very long nose and very huge ears and tiny, tiny eyes and she spoke *very loud*.

"You must be de piple dat found my vallet!"

She held Madame's head in her shaky hands, brought Madame's cheeks close to her mouth, and planted a nice, loud kiss.

Madame smiled but quickly straightened up. She told me to give the old woman her wallet, which I did. Well, what do you know I got in return? A mitzvah, for sure, but also a nice, loud kiss on my cheek. And it was a wet one too. I tried not to let the old woman see how I wiped it off while she *bensched* us: "G-tt bless you, G-tt bless you!"

As we were leaving, the old woman called, "Vait, vait!" We turned and she said, "Tell me, maybe you can help me find my cat too?"

"Cat? As in *chat?*" Madame asked.

"Sha? What? Are you telling me to be quiet? And I tought dat you vere so kind!"

Madame Chamberlaine embraced the old woman. "Never mind. Tell me more about your cat."

"Vell, my cat, Yentele, she helps me cetch de mice in mine house."

"So where is Yentele now?" Madame asked.

"Gone. One minute she's here and de next minute she's gone. Can you help me find her? You found my vallet."

We looked at Madame Chamberlaine. She smiled. "*Bien sûr*. We will certainly try."

"I need her quickly." The old lady lowered her voice. "You see, I caught a mouse and trapped it under a soup plate in de kitchen. I need Yentele to get rid of it."

Ew. Shuly and I looked at each other. *We had better get out of this house ASAP.*

Madame gave me a wink. "We'll be back, Mrs. Podhertzer. *Be'ezras Hashem* with your *cha*—I mean your cat."

We scrambled out.

"Madame, we don't even know what the cat looks like. And this city is massive. How are we supposed to find it?"

"Let's look around the house and we'll take it from there."

Madame, her pink fluffy scarf wrapped around her shoulders, poked little holes in the fresh snow with her heels. She walked to the back of Mrs. Podhertzer's house. She checked under the stairs and on the back porch, behind a wooden board and in a small shed. She stopped and stood very still.

"*Écoutez.*"

We had no idea what she said, but we stood and then we heard it.

"Meow…"

"That sounds like Mrs. Podhertzer's cat."

We laughed and Madame moved closer to the sound. It was coming from an overturned clay plant holder. We followed her and suddenly saw white and brown fur. Was the cat hurt?

We stood over the pot as Madame bent low.

"*Oh là là!* Look, babies."

Sure enough, Yentele had three kittens! All white and brown and so, so small.

Madame went back to Mrs. Podhertzer (we refused to go inside, as we were not especially fond of mice) and told her the news.

"A *nes*!" she yelled. "Now I'll have four cats to take care of mine mice!"

She gave Madame a basket that she lined with a towel. And Madame, who didn't know how to be scared of anything (maybe they don't have a word in French for "scared"), picked up Yentele and her babies and put them into the snug basket. Mrs. Podhertzer was thrilled when Madame handed it over. I think the whole city must have heard her yelling her thanks.

Madame smiled and said, "*Bien sûr*, Mrs. Podhertzer. Next time you lose something, you'll know whom to call."

Fun with FOREIGN WORDS

alors	So
chat	Cat
chocolat chaud	Hot chocolate
écoutez	Listen
neige	Snow
oui	Yes
s'il vous plait	Please
trois	Three
DO YOU REMEMBER THESE?	
bien sûr	Certainly
chèrie	Dear
oui	Yes

The Power of the Flower

My brother Donny was having his bar mitzvah and it was going to be a triple whammy of excitement. Donny was the oldest, which meant that his was the first major *simchah* we kids would be participating in fully, and we planned on pulling out all the stops. Us girls were busy worrying about all the usual stuff girls must discuss over and over again—shoes, hair, dresses.

Donny donned his new hat every single day to make sure it fit right. (I had thought that trying on stuff like every three seconds was something reserved for girls. Maybe I was missing something.) We teased him that we'll sneak a flower on the hatband on the night of the bar mitzvah. Oh boy, the look on his face when we said that—scary stuff! So we let him be and went back to our own flowers, the flowers for our hair. Shuly and I were going to wear matching velvet dresses and we'd have these gorgeous peach and ivory flowers in our hair. The flowers had crystals and pearls, and looked absolutely stunning. I wouldn't think about sharing them with Donny's hat, not even for a joke.

Oh, and of course Madame Chamberlaine would be coming to the bar mitzvah too.

The grand night finally, finally arrived and by four o'clock I was ready to leave. The bar mitzvah wouldn't start before eight. I ran around the house trying to hurry things along, but just ended up getting under my mother's feet. She got annoyed and I got insulted because I was only trying to help, and Donny yelled because he couldn't remember where he had put his hat.

"No, no, don't go blaming me," I cried. "I didn't hide it to slip the flower inside. Promise!" But Donny thought so and chased me around the house until I said that I heard the photographer coming and I'd insist he take a video of the scene.

Madame came in just then. That woman doesn't need words to help her understand things.

"*Chèrie!*" She smiled as she stretched her hand out to me.

"Where are we going?" I asked her.

"Is Shuly ready?"

I nodded.

"*Merveilleux!* We're going to invite someone special to the bar mitzvah."

Shuly and I looked at each other.

"Madame, we already sent the invitations to everyone on the list."

She clucked her tongue. "We must invite one more person. Do you want to go?"

"With you? Of course!"

"*Non, non.* Not with *moi.* By yourselves. I must go somewhere else and will not have time to invite her."

"Uh…we want to go with you."

"I know, *chèries,* but I must go by myself. *Mais,* I will walk you to where the lady lives. Okay?"

We nodded, not sure what we were getting ourselves into.

We slipped on our coats (I tried wiggling my way out of wearing one over my beautiful dress, but Madame gave me a wink and I knew I better not fight it!) and set off in the frigid weather. It was so cold out that I was too busy blowing on my fingers to see where Madame was leading us. When she stopped I looked up in surprise. Huh? The old age home?

"*Voilà,*" Madame said happily. "You need to find Madame Cohen in room 308. Tell her that I arranged for someone to pick her up at seven thirty. Be kind, *mes chèries.* She is quite sad." And she was off, her pink skirt and tassels swirling in the wind.

"Okay, *ma chèrie,*" I mimicked Madame to Shuly. "I think that I give you the full honor of finding Madame Cohen."

"I think, *ma chèrie,* that we better do this together. Otherwise Madame Cohen will give us one look and we'll wither away."

We laughed and swung the glass door open. We climbed the steps until we reached the third floor. 304, 306…aha, there it was…308. The door was closed. We rapped. No answer. We knocked louder. Still no answer.

"You think we should try the door?"

Shuly shrugged. She looked scared.

"You scared or something, *ma chèrie*?" I asked, trying to be funny but so afraid myself.

"*Moi?* Never!" she declared.

"Good. So please, maybe you can open the door?"

Shuly gulped. "Are you serious? I'm scared."

"What do you think is hiding inside? Elephants? Lions? Dinosaurs?"

"No. Just one very old lady, with pointy ears and sharp teeth…"

"…and razor-like nails and fire in her eyes… Oh come on! What are we scared of? *Un, deux, trois*, open!"

We pushed the door open and looked inside.

The room was narrow, long, and very neat. There was a little square table along one wall. Behind that, there was a stainless steel sink, a black counter, a small burner, and a microwave. Red curtains were hanging from the window over the counter. Pushed against the other wall was a bed. The sheets were red and flowery, and an old, wrinkled woman lay on it snoring softly.

"Do you see the lions?" I whispered to Shuly.

She smiled. "No, but I do see a wheelchair, which means she can't be too healthy. Let's wait until she wakes up."

We waited and waited until we saw one eye sliding open. Madame Cohen's eyebrows were cross and her lips were in a scowl.

"Hello, Madame Cohen. We came to tell you that Madame Chamberlaine wants you to come to our bar mitzvah today. Someone will come and get you at seven thirty."

"*Quoi?* Says who? I will not come, as I told that Chamberlaine already."

We shrugged, waved, and ran out. We saw why Madame didn't want to come herself. Smart woman, she knew that Madame Cohen would refuse.

We raced back home and promptly forgot about Madame Cohen because then my mother really did need my help, so I was busy, busy, busy until we left for the hall.

All my neighbors and aunts and uncles and just about every adult in the neighborhood was there. It was such fun flitting through the hall, getting a gazillion mazal tovs from people that I didn't even know and having a fabulous time with my cousins. I nearly collided with a wheelchair at one point and quickly apologized.

Shuly whispered, "She came, Madame Cohen, see? But she still looks mad."

I ran to tell Madame Chamberlaine and she spoke to Madame Cohen in French gibberish. Madame settled the old woman at a table. We pranced off before Madame could make us sit beside her.

At one point, I think when the waiters brought out the dessert, I put my hand on my hair and realized that—hey! My beautiful flowers were gone. They must have fallen out as I was running around.

I looked under the table. Some napkins and lots of crumbs were all I saw.

"Shuly, can you help me find the flowers?" I asked.

We looked all over, but they were nowhere. We even checked the kitchen area, but the flowers weren't there either.

"Maybe Donny decided that he does want a flower in his hat after all," I said with a giggle. But no, his hat was smooth and black and flowerless.

I heard quick steps behind me. I turned to see Madame Chamberlaine in her pink heels. Her eyes were shiny, her cheeks rosy, and she was trying hard not to laugh.

She looked at my hair and smiled. "Aha, I thought that it must be you."

She took my hand in her own. "*Viens, ma chèrie*, you have made someone very, very *contente!*"

"*Contente?*"

"Happy, *ma petite.*"

I wasn't sure what she meant.

"I see that you're missing flowers in your hair," she said.

"Well, yeah. I can't find them."

Madame laughed, that tinkling, delightful sound. "Aha, I have found them."

"You did?"

"Come see."

We walked to a side table and there, sitting in her wheel-chair, was Madame Cohen with a wide smile on her face.

"She looks happy," I said.

"Do you see why? Look at her suit."

I smiled. In each of her buttonholes was a peach or ivory flower, shiny with crystals and pearls.

"How did they get there?" I asked.

Madame shrugged. "*Vraiment, je ne sais pas.* But it seems to make her happy. Do you want the flowers back?"

I shook my head. "No way, and make her mad again? I'd rather remain flowerless like Donny, *merci beaucoup!*"

Fun with FOREIGN WORDS

ontente	Happy
je ne sais pas	I don't know
mais	But
merci beaucoup	Thank you very much
merveilleux	Marvelous
voilà	Here you go

DO YOU REMEMBER THESE?

chèrie	Dear
moi	Me
non	No
quoi	What
vraiment	Really
quoi	What

The Surprising Costume

Shuly and I were excited, and not your regular "ha-ha" excited either. Not only was Purim coming, Madame Chamberlaine promised to come for the holiday too! And this time, we had a surprise for her.

You see, Shuly and I decided to shock Madame with a smashing costume of our own. I know you're just drooling to know what it was. It was pink and came with heels and frilly scarves and tassels on the kerchief… Yup! Shuly and I would be dressing up as Madame Chamberlaine!

Boy, would Madame be flabbergasted to see herself in two smaller versions.

I spoke to her the week before, and she said she would be at our house on Taanis Esther. If she'd get delayed, she wouldn't be later than five or six o'clock. She also said that she'd surprise us. That's when Shuly and I thought that this time we would knock Madame off her feet. (That's just an expression; of course we never could knock her off and I'm not sure I would dare try!)

Purim in our house is a community affair. My father reads the Megillah in our dining room and every mother with little children and every elderly person who can't make it to shul, and everyone's grandmother's cousin ends up around our dining room table. We're quite crammed, of course, but it's fun and this year was going to be much more fun with Madame there. She was sure to put some extra Purim spirit into the gathering.

It was Taanis Esther, and Shuly and I jumped every time the doorbell rang. Twelve o'clock, one o'clock... We were getting edgy. Where was Madame Chamberlaine?

"Don't worry," my mother said with a smile. "She promised she'd be here."

Two o'clock, three o'clock, four o'clock...

"Ma, this can't be. I hope she didn't miss her flight."

My mother looked worried. "I certainly hope not."

We went back to our seats by the living room window. Cars came, people came, even *mishloach manos* arrived at our door, but no Madame. My mother told us to get ready for Purim. Usually we were so excited to dress up. My brothers ran to get their swords and mustaches, and Shuly and I forced ourselves to go upstairs to change. We felt like such flops dressing up as Madame Chamberlaine when she wasn't even around to see the costumes.

As soon as we draped the bright pink kerchiefs over our

heads and slipped into the heels, we started to feel *Purimdig* and a tad better. When my mother applied pink makeup to our lips and cheeks, we felt giddy and happy. Madame would surely show up.

"Did she come yet?" Shuly asked my father when we came downstairs.

He shook his head. "No, but I'm going to shul to daven and hear the Megillah. Want to come along?"

Shuly and I looked at each other. Neither of us wanted to miss Madame's arrival. But maybe she wouldn't come after all? We decided to stay home. If she did come, we wanted to be there to say hello.

Our house started filling up. Old Mrs. Perel came with her granddaughter. She took the seat closest to the door as she did every year. Our neighbor Mrs. Donut came with her flock of children all dressed up as...you guessed it...doughnuts! One had sprinkles, one chocolate, and another jelly. Mrs. Gruen came in her wheelchair. Usually, one of us had to wheel her in and back home, but this time she came with a helper. Shuly and I weren't sure if the helper was dressed up or was for real; she certainly looked foreign. Mrs. Gelb came with her grandson who was dressed up as a British soldier. We laughed when the tall fur hat kept slipping past his nose. More and more people came; the noise was loud and the air was stuffy.

Mrs. Perel motioned us over. "What are you dressed up as, a lady?" she asked.

We shook our heads. "Not just any lady. We're dressed up as Madame Chamberlaine."

Mrs. Gruen, who was sitting next to Mrs. Perel, said, "Who? I've never heard of anybody with such a strange name."

Her helper nodded. "*Si, si,* I have an *amiga* and her *nombre* is also Chamberlily."

Shuly giggled.

Mrs. Gruen patted her helper's hand. "You're so special. You helped me so nicely."

"*Si, si, de nada.*" Her helper smiled, showing two rows of bright white teeth. She wore a red hat, a blue dress, and red shoes with big blue flowers.

So this woman was for real.

Finally, we heard my father's booming voice at the doorway. "A *freilichen* Purim, everybody!"

The old women all nodded and answered. The little kids hid behind their mothers' skirts. My father placed his *megillah* on the table and got ready to read.

I poked Shuly with my elbow. "Madame isn't here yet," I whispered.

Shuly's eyes looked sad. "She promised." Her voice sounded like there were tears somewhere inside.

I looked down. She did promise. *Why isn't Madame here yet?*

After the Megillah was read, everyone began piling out of the house. I was able to see the dining room walls again. Mrs. Perel and Mrs. Gruen stayed to eat at our house.

Shuly and I were beginning to grumble. Purim was supposed to be a whole lot of fun; why didn't Madame come already?

"Girls, it's Purim," my father said. "Why the long faces? C'mon boys!" He grabbed my brothers' hands and began to sing and dance. The two old women and the Spanish helper clapped along.

"Happy now?" my father asked as he gave the boys one last twirl around the room.

We smiled. We sure wanted Madame with us on such a wonderful day, but we could still be happy even if she was delayed, and hey, the day wasn't over until it was over and she could show up any minute. And how amazed she would be to see us in her clothes!

We went to help my mother serve the food. She made tri-colored challah, a whole, huge smoked fish (my favorite), and mashed potatoes shaped like hamantaschen (she put mushroom sauce where the jam would go). We spoke, we made the old women laugh, and the Spanish helper turned out to be a lot of fun. She spoke to us in Spanish and taught us to count to ten. (Don't try it until you practice rolling those r's: *uno, dos, tres, cuatro, cinco, seis, siete, ocho, nueve, diez*.) She helped us clear the table and told us jokes.

We didn't forget about Madame. We watched the door all night out of the corners of our eyes and my mother tried calling her cell phone, which didn't ring.

We told Mrs. Perel and Mrs. Gruen and her helper about Madame and they all wanted to meet her. They waited and waited too, but she still didn't come. We saw the three women yawning. The Spanish woman helped the two ladies get their coats on, and she started wheeling Mrs. Gruen out.

"Oh," I said to her. "We've had such fun, but you haven't even told us your name."

She turned to look at me and winked. "*Vraiment*, do you not know who I am?"

I stared at her. "No way..."

"I surprised you, didn't I?"

"Oh, Madame. You were here all along!"

"*Bien sûr*. I promised that I would come, didn't I?" She

smiled at Shuly and me. "I love your costumes. You two look more like me than I do!"

Mrs. Perel and Mrs. Gruen both watched in amazement. "So you were that *amiga* Chamberlily all along," Mrs. Gruen said with a wink.

Madame's laughter tinkled through the happy night. We went along with her to take the two women home, then she came back to our house and gave each of us a pink wrapped box of her tasty pastries.

"*Muchas gracias,*" I told her.

She laughed and said to me, "So, Madame Chamberlaine, how do we say *Purim* in French?"

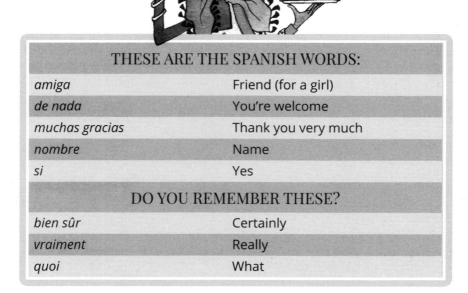

Fun with FOREIGN WORDS

THESE ARE THE SPANISH WORDS:	
amiga	Friend (for a girl)
de nada	You're welcome
muchas gracias	Thank you very much
nombre	Name
si	Yes
DO YOU REMEMBER THESE?	
bien sûr	Certainly
vraiment	Really
quoi	What

Clowning Around

I pulled the colorful wig on and glanced in the mirror. "How do I look?"

Shuly was busy stuffing the tips of the super-long shoes she was wearing.

"Wow, awesome. I love your makeup."

"Sis, look in the mirror. Madame Chamberlaine did your makeup exactly like mine."

She peeked into the mirror just as Madame came flitting down the steps.

"*Chèries*, are you ready?"

We both stared at her.

"*Quoi?*" she asked when she noticed that we weren't talking and just looking.

"You…you mean you're also dressed as a clown?"

"And why not?" she asked.

"Well…I don't know…well…yeah, why not?"

"Why not, indeed," she said. "Get your coats on and *on y va*!"

"Nuh-uh, we don't do coats on Purim," Shuly said. "There are plenty of pillows anyway under our costumes."

Madame Chamberlaine shrugged. "*Bien*, so let's shake a leg." She collected all the *mishloach manos* that we had prepared and we ran off. We were going to visit the sick children in the hospital. Madame had realized that the poor children had no one to cheer them up on Purim and no one who would bring them *mishloach manos* either. So she asked us to join her; how could we not agree?

We stopped by the information desk to ask which floor the pediatric ward was on. The woman stared at us.

"*Quoi?*" Shuly and I giggled.

"What exactly are you doing here in those costumes?" she asked.

"It's Purim today," Madame explained, "and we came to cheer the children up."

She shrugged. "Sixth floor."

When the elevator door opened, there was barely space for us to squeeze in. We managed, though. The doors closed and we stared.

"Now, *quoi*?" I whispered to Shuly.

We giggled again. In the elevator, squished next to like a million people, were two more clowns.

Madame smiled. "Looks like we weren't the only ones with this brilliant idea."

All of a sudden, the lights in the elevator went off.

"What is this, a Purim joke?" I asked.

Everyone else was quiet like a stone.

Then…

"Ahhhh!"

Everyone started yelling at once. The elevator wasn't moving and the lit numbers telling us which floor we were up to were dead too.

"*Oh là là*," I heard Madame say.

Someone had the bright idea of turning on the flashlight on his phone, so in under ten seconds, little flashlights shone from everyone's hands. I was scared stiff when I realized that we were in no Purim shpiel. It was a broken elevator, for real! And there was no air coming in either.

Did I mention that we were stuffed like sardines in there?

But at least we were able to see, so that we wouldn't step on anyone else's toes or put our hands into someone else's pocket. (Who am I kidding—it was nice to look at everyone's worried faces to know that I wasn't the only scaredy-cat around!)

As we were closest to the elevator buttons, Madame pressed the Help button.

Nothing.

The yelling began again.

"Okay, everyone stay calm," someone said. It was one of the other clowns in the elevator.

"So nice to see you all dressed up with the same idea we had," Madame said to her.

"Idea?" said the clown.

"Yes, you know, dressed up for Purim," Madame explained.

"Purim?"

"Yes, Purim."

"What's that?" one clown asked.

Madame looked at us and then at the clowns. "You are dressed up, are you not?"

The clowns nodded.

"And it's because of Purim, no?"

"Pardon?" said the clown. "I lost you. What does *Purim* mean?"

Madame laughed. All the passengers in the elevator turned to stare at her. "*Oh là là!* This is so funny. You must be medical clowns."

"Why yes, we are. Aren't you?"

"Why, no! We're dressed up for Purim, you know, our holiday. We came to cheer up the children."

"Exactly what we do as well," said the clown. She gestured to a girl in a wheelchair. "We're bringing her back up to the sixth floor." The clown leaned over the girl and said, "But hey, Gittel, looks like we're playing spooky house for a bit."

Gittel didn't smile.

"We're trying to find Gittel's smile," one clown, with blue hair and pointy ears, said. "She lost her smile a long, long time ago and we can't seem to find it anywhere. Oh look, Gittel."

The clown pretended to pull something out of her ear. "I finally found it!" She stuck the pretend smile on Gittel's lips.

Gittel didn't think it was too funny, because she didn't even crack a smirk.

"You mean this girl never laughs?" Madame asked in shock.

All the people in the squishy elevator stared at the poor child.

"Never."

"Wow," was heard from all sides.

"Hey, girlie," one man yelled from the other side of the lift. "Where does the boat go when he's not feeling well? To the dock! Ha, ha!"

"Oh, I got a good one too," a lady with a huge purse said. "What do you get when you shake up a cow?"

Nobody answered.

"Milkshake!"

Gittel didn't smile. I did, though.

"Ooh, ooh, I have one," a woman with a coffee in her hand said. "Knock, knock. Who's there? Adore. Adore who? Adore—*a door*—is between us; why don't you open it?"

"Knock, knock," someone yelled from the corner. "Who's there? Don't. Don't who? Don't you guys remember that we're in an elevator and we're stuck?"

The elevator became very quiet.

"*Mais oui*," Madame said. "We must do something about this."

Gittel shrieked. "*Tu parle français?*"

Madame bent toward Gittel. "*Oui, chèrie. Toi aussi?*"

"No way," Gittel said. "Don't tell me that you're… Madame Chamberlaine!"

"She sure is," I said.

Gittel stared.

"*Quoi?*" Shuly and I said together with a laugh.

"I read all your stories and I so badly wanted to meet you. *Oh là là!* I did! I just did!"

And of course, you know what happened next. Gittel gave

the most wonderful, happiest laugh anyone in the stuck elevator had ever heard!

The medical clowns stood there scratching their colorful wigs and—*bang, bang, bang*. The door slid open and a man in overalls stood in front of us.

"My, my. I've never seen such a calm group after they've been stuck in an elevator for so long."

We all laughed and walked out.

"Hey, hey! Wait up, everyone." We turned to look at Gittel. She was still smiling and said, "Knock, knock! Who's there? Orange. Orange who? Orange you glad we're finally out of the elevator?"

We laughed again, and then went to make some more children happy.

Fun with FOREIGN WORDS

bien	Good
mais oui	Why, yes
on y va	Let's go
toi aussi	You also
tu parle français	You speak French

DO YOU REMEMBER THESE?

| *chèrie* | Dear |
| *oui* | Yes |

Madame in a Tree

"Madame Chamberlaine, where are we going now?"

Madame, as usual, was way ahead of us.

"We're going to find *cerises*," she said in a pleasant singsong.

Shuly and I looked at each other as we huffed to catch up to our friend.

"Find who?"

Madame stopped rushing and turned to face us. "Not who. What."

"So what are we finding?" I dared to ask.

She tapped her pink heel on the black pavement. "*Cerises*. Now come along."

She twirled around, the fringes on her *tichel* swiping my

face, and marched forward. I grabbed her hand. She held out her other hand for Shuly.

"You two must learn to hurry up. At the rate you're going, Mashiach will be here by the time we even get to the market."

"So we're finding Suri's what?" I tried again.

"*Mes petites*, Suri lost nothing and we're going to find *cerises*. That's cherries."

"But haven't you heard, Madame, that it's not cherry season yet?"

"So I've heard." She didn't even let us stop to catch our breath. "We're going to the farmers' market. Maybe we'll find some there. *Mes petites*, I must make cherry jam before I leave for France."

"Cherry jam? For us?"

"Non, *chéries*. It's for Mrs. Pinto. But I will let you taste some."

"Mmm, sounds good," we decided. We skipped along.

When we got to the farmers' market, there were no cherries in the stalls. But Madame would not give up. She went to every farmer and asked, "Monsieur, do you have cherries for me today?"

And they all answered, "Sorry, they aren't ripe yet."

"Ripe, shmipe," we heard her mumble. "I must have *cerises*."

Finally, one farmer with a large straw hat and washed-out green overalls had pity on her. "Look, lady, my wife Zelda and I own a huge farm. Do you know Zelda? Heh, I say she's the boss of all our animals, because the sheep and cows will listen only to her!"

"Hmm, Zelda? You don't mean Zelda Peppo, do you?" Madame asked.

"I most certainly do. Zelda, Zelda!"

A woman with a floppy white hat waved. Then she saw Madame and ran over.

"Oh, my dear! You haven't aged a day since seventh grade. You do remember how we loved that boarding school in England, don't you?" She hugged Madame. "You must come to our farm to meet all my lovely chickens."

"Well," Madame said with a smile. "We are quite desperate for cherries. If you have some in your farm, we'll come."

"Delightful! We'll finish off here and then we'll be off."

Madame's cheeks became pink like two roses. She turned to us. "*Mes petites*, do you want to come?"

"Do we ever!"

When the farmer and his wife were finished selling their products, we climbed into the back of their red pickup truck. Madame took out two large pink scarves from her bag and wrapped each one around our heads so the wind wouldn't whip our faces and hair. The farmer drove down a long, long road. There were vast light green fields everywhere we looked. The air smelled like fruit and hay and horses.

Finally, the truck stopped and we all jumped out.

Zelda showed us her chickens. That wasn't too exciting as I don't really like the smell of chickens. Then, she took us to the cherry trees.

"I must go now," she said. "It was a pleasure seeing you again, Madame Chamberlaine. Make sure to keep in touch. And happy picking!"

"Tell me," Madame asked before the Peppos walked off, "where can I find the ripe cherries?"

The farmer laughed. "Well, I hope you'll find some. Try the very top of the tree first."

"I see," Madame said.

"How will she get to the top of any of these trees?" Shuly whispered. "They look huge."

Madame sniffed the air. "Ahh... Smell the *cerises, mes petites.*" She grabbed a wooden ladder that was leaning against a tree and moved it to the largest one. She climbed on and reached for a cluster of tiny cherries, and opened one with her fingers.

"Wow, these are hard like rocks. They will never do."

We heard a creak, and watched in horror as a large crack appeared in the middle of the wooden ladder.

"Madame, careful!" we yelled.

In a flash, Madame Chamberlaine grabbed on to a branch. She heaved herself to a strong part and when I looked again, she was standing, with her high heels on the branch, checking each twig of cherries. She kept going higher and higher until she was almost on the very top branch!

"Be careful, Madame," we yelled again as we peered through the green foliage.

Madame parted a branch and looked down at us. "Don't worry about me," she called.

We watched her check each cluster and then heard, "*Oui, oui.*"

"We?" I looked at Shuly. "What should 'we' do?"

Shuly thought. "Doesn't *oui* mean 'yes'?"

"You're right, I forgot. So that means that she found ripe cherries. But how will she come out of the tree?"

"Do you think we should call the farmer?"

We watched Madame trying to climb lower with a few

clusters of cherries in her hand. We were sure that her high heels and frilly pink sweater were not the right gear for climbing off trees.

"Madame, do you want to throw us the cherries so it'll be easier for you to come down?"

"Throw them? *Non, non.* They will get bruised."

She stood on a branch. We saw the branch underneath far below her; how would she manage to come down? She stepped a little toward the edge of the branch, a little more, and more…then we saw her sway back and forth. The branch began to shake a tiny bit, harder, and even harder…

"Madame, you're falling!"

We ran like the wind to get the farmer. He roared back in his tractor with a ladder perched across his shoulder.

But when we got to the tree, Madame was no longer on it. She was standing next to it, her heels still on her feet and the clusters of plump, juicy cherries in her hand.

"Where did you run off to, *mes petites?*"

Shuly and I looked at each other and at the farmer. He shrugged. "I guess that was a close call."

"Madame," we said in shock, "how did you get down so fast with no ladder?"

"Tsk, tsk. I did and that's that."

She paid for the cherries and we caught a taxi back to our house.

When we woke up the next morning, the house smelled like…cherries. I dressed quickly and flew down the steps. Sure enough, Madame Chamberlaine was standing over the stove and stirring a pot.

"*Bonjour*," I greeted her. "You promised us a taste."

"*Bien sûr*." She dished out a generous spoonful and spread it on a piece of toast. "*Bon appetite*."

Yummy stuff. Madame prepared a cherry jam sandwich for me to take to school.

When we visited elderly Mrs. Pinto, she ate the entire container of jam in one sitting!

"So I guess it was worth gong to the farm and getting stuck in the tree to make Mrs. Pinto happy?" I asked Madame.

"*Bien sûr, bien sûr, chaque minute*."

Fun with FOREIGN WORDS

bonjour	Good day, hi, hello
chaque minute	Every minute
DO YOU REMEMBER THESE?	
bien sûr	Certainly
chèrie	Dear
mes petites	My little ones
non	No
oui	Yes

Visiting Miss Kokosh

S o where are we off to today?" I asked as I struggled to keep up with Madame Chamberlaine's tall pink shoes.

"To Miss Kokosh. Hurry along because she is quite upset about something."

Shuly and I looked at each other. Miss Kokosh? What kind of a name was that?

But if Madame was going to her, she must have been somebody worth visiting. We ran faster.

Madame stopped in front of an eight-foot-high purple fence.

"Wow, this is unusual," I said as I looked through the slats. Inside, the front lawn was popping with colorful flowers almost as tall as me. Fake flamingos were scattered all over, some on one foot and some in the middle of dancing.

Madame pushed the gate open and walked up the cobble-stoned pathway. We reached a bright yellow door.

"I thought Miss Kokosh would have a brown door or at least a cinnamon-smelling door," Shuly said.

Madame smiled and pulled a long, tasseled rope. We heard the bell chime inside.

The door opened and there was Miss Kokosh. Honest opinion, right? Well, she looked like a kokosh cake. I mean her hair looked like a kokosh cake. It was tied tightly in a bun, half-white, half-black. Just like a chocolate-vanilla cake.

She was nice and plump, with rosy cheeks and small, chubby fingers. She stood on her tiptoes to hug Madame and showed us inside. We sat on a zebra-striped couch and Miss Kokosh brought us, what else? Kokosh cake and cinnamon tea.

"*Délicieux!* The best kokosh cake on the planet," Madame said as she took a bite.

Our hostess looked pleased. "I'm not called Miss Kokosh for nothing, eh?"

"So, Miss Kokosh," Madame said after her cake and tea were safely on the table. "What's the problem?"

Her jolly eyes looked frightened. "Madame Chamberlaine, it's terrible, the noises. I'm scared enough to sleep on my own every night. But with these terrible noises, I want to run away!"

Madame clucked her tongue. "Tell me more."

"Every night, as I lie in my bed, I hear terrible shrieking. First I thought that it was the neighbors, but they say it's not them. I'm terribly frightened. I stay up all night, shivering and shaking, hoping that whatever is making all that noise won't decide to visit me in my bedroom. Can you please, please help me?"

"Hmm," Madame said as she tied her pink frilly scarf tighter around her neck. "Interesting."

"No, Madame. This is certainly not interesting. It's scary," Miss Kokosh said.

She was right. I strained my ears to hear the sounds, but all was still.

Madame put a pointy finger to her forehead and was silent. None of us made a peep. Finally, she stood up and said, "Is there an attic or something here?"

Miss Kokosh nodded. "A little one. I haven't been up there in years."

"I suppose you don't mind if I take a peek, do you?"

"Why sure, you can go. But I'm not coming with you."

Madame turned to us. "*Et vous, mes petites?*"

I shrugged.

"*Non?*" she asked gently.

"I'll come if you promise me that I'll be back down in five minutes," I said.

"*Très bien. Viens.*" She held out her hand and I probably squeezed all the blood out of her fingers because, folks, I was scared. *Oh là là!*

Miss Kokosh opened a creaky wooden closet door. Inside was a wooden ladder. Madame's shoes clicked on the rungs as she climbed up. She reached the top and looked down.

"Coming, *chèrie?*"

Slowly, I climbed after her. I was right behind her as she slowly pushed open the trap door. And I saw them. Oh boy, did I see them. Tens and tens of them hanging upside-down.

"Aaaahhhh!!!" I yelled as I tripped down the ladder, falling and stumbling until I reached the living room.

"What? What happened up there?" Shuly asked.

I heard Madame's heels tapping the floor. "*Exactement* as I thought."

"What?" Shuly asked again. "Tell me already."

I looked at Miss Kokosh. She was sitting on an armchair, her eyes closed and her body tight and stiff.

Madame followed my gaze. She walked over to Miss Kokosh and put an arm around her. "Come, *chèrie*. I'll take you back with me to their house for a bit until I take care of the problem." Miss Kokosh stood up and got her coat. We all trekked out, with me the happiest of all to be out of that house.

"Tell me already," Shuly hissed. "What did you see in the attic?"

"You'll never believe this," I whispered back. "There were tons of bats up there. It looked like a spooky house!"

"Eww. Gross."

"You betcha. Poor Miss Kokosh. I sure am glad that I don't sleep in that house."

"You watch out, because you never know what Madame Chamberlaine has up her sleeve."

"She had better not make me sleep there." I shivered.

"Oh, *chèrie*." I heard Madame's voice coming from behind me. "I wouldn't be that cruel. But I will need your help."

Oh no!

We came home. While my mother set Miss Kokosh up by the kitchen counter to bake one of her super-duper chocolate babkas, Madame motioned for me to follow her.

She took me back outside. "*Chèrie*, I know this will be hard, but we need to get rid of the bats tonight. Will you help me?"

"Really? I'm so scared of them, I'll probably faint if I see them again."

"All I need you to do is stay outside and tell me when you see them flying out."

I nodded.

We walked back to Miss Kokosh's house. Madame held my hand and told me that a bat eats between two and four thousand insects a night. (That's like a kid eating twenty pizza pies in one sitting!)

Bats fly out at dusk to feed and fly back at dawn. Madame waited to see the colony fly out, then she crept back into the attic. By herself. She asked me to see if more bats were flying out. I did see more, then even more, and yes, I must admit that I was hiding behind bushes as I looked. Then I thought that I was seeing things, because with Madame Chamberlaine you can never be sure. But there she was, strutting around on the roof of the house, in her heels, no less. I don't know what she did but I was waiting for her a long, long time. Finally, she came down. How? I haven't the foggiest clue. (Maybe she flew down!) She held my hand and we went back home.

The house smelled like cinnamon and chocolate and I knew without a doubt that Miss Kokosh deserved every letter in her last name. We ate and then walked her back home.

The next morning, the phone rang before we left to school. It was Miss Kokosh.

"I slept like a baby last night," she said. "Thank you, thank you!"

Madame smiled. "*Avec plaisir.*" She hung up and said, "I

sure hope those bats don't come back, because I'm not sure if I want to do that again."

We laughed and sat down to a breakfast of chocolate kokosh cake.

Fun with FOREIGN WORDS

avec plaisir	With pleasure
délicieux	Delicious
et vous	And you
exactement	Exactly

DO YOU REMEMBER THESE?

chèrie	Dear
mes petites	My little ones
non	No
très bien	Very well
viens	Come

The Gigantic Sea Monster

I was curled up on the couch, phone in hand, talking to Madame Chamberlaine.

"So, Madame, did you hear what we have here in our lake?"

"*Non, chèrie.* Tell me."

"You'll never believe this, but there's this huge, huge fish or whale or shark or something swimming around in the water and no one knows how it got there. The fishermen are petrified to fish in the lake. No one knows what to do. It's scary." I shivered.

"Baloney and fish sticks!" Madame laughed. "A whale cannot appear all of a sudden."

"But people saw it! They even have pictures of it. People are scared to go outside."

Madame's laugh sounded like a bell ringing. "*Tu raconte des bêtises.*"

"Well, Madame, I'm not sure what that means, but I imagine that you don't believe me. But you're not here, so you don't really know. I'm telling you, we're all so scared of what this is and what it can do to us."

Of course she laughed again. Well, what did she know? She was far away and couldn't feel the fear we were living with at every moment. How did the sea creature get into the lake and what was it? Could it be the *livyasan*? That would be exciting, but we all knew, just knew, that it was something a lot more sinister than that.

A day passed, then two. Shuly and I would creep to the lake to steal a quick peek at the huge mound that streaked across. Then, frightened and breathless, we ran home and locked ourselves behind our door.

One day after school, I came home to a familiar smell. The kitchen counters were covered with trays of pastries and cake.

"Ma?"

My mother smiled. Behind her stood Madame Chamberlaine.

"Oh, Madame!" I hugged her tightly. "You came!"

Her nose dusted with flour, she hugged me back. "*Chèrie,* so good to see you again."

"Why did you come?'

She smiled. "I missed you."

She popped a sugar cookie into my fingers. "Here, make a *berachah.*"

Yum!

She untied her apron and took my hands in hers. "Is homework done?" I nodded. "*Bien. On est prêts, alors!*"

I stared at her. "What?"

"Let's say it like the Americans do: We're ready to roll!"

"Where to?" I asked.

"We're going to find the *monstre marin*."

I think I knew what she meant before I even understood the words she used in French. No way no how was I going anywhere near that lake. With Madame we wouldn't just take a peek and run back home. She would take us *into* the water!

I shook my head.

"Well then, I guess I'll be going myself. Shuly?" Madame turned to her. Would she agree to go along?

Shuly looked at me, then at Madame, then at my mother. She shrugged her shoulders.

Phew, she wasn't going either. So I wasn't the only scaredy-cat around.

Madame draped a fuzzy pink sweater over her shoulders. "So long, *mes petites*. I'll let you know what monster I found in the water." She opened the front door and disappeared.

Shuly and I stared at each other. We couldn't let her go by herself. What if the shark attacked her and nobody would be there to save her? We grabbed our jackets and ran after her pink silhouette.

"Madame! Madame! Wait up!"

She smiled as her feet continued moving quickly. "Ah, you decided to come. To save me from the monster, I suppose."

We both laughed nervously.

We reached the lake, which was empty. Then we saw the

grey hump bobbing along the water.

"There, Madame! There it is. Do you see it?"

"Hmph. I sure do."

Madame walked briskly across the rocks and stopped at the edge, where there was a little overturned rowboat. She flipped it over. It used to be green, but the paint was peeling and it looked old and very, very fragile.

"You mean you're planning to go into the water in *that*?" I asked.

Madame nodded. "And you're coming with me."

I gasped.

She smiled. "Otherwise who will save me from the shark?"

I dropped my face into my trembling hands. Oh no, no! She couldn't be serious. She was going to take us into the water with that huge "thing" in a rickety, old boat? I was ready to go home.

But Madame didn't look the least bit concerned. She hummed as she found the two oars and pushed the boat into the water.

"Coming?" she called.

Shuly shuffled to the water. Did I have a choice?

Shivering and terribly scared, I followed them. Madame lifted me into the bobbing boat, then placed Shuly beside me. *It had better not float away without Madame in it!* But she made it in and swiftly and easily rowed to the center of the lake.

"Hmm… Anyone see the creature yet?"

We looked around as we cowered lower into the hard bench.

"There!" Shuly yelled.

And sure enough the tremendous mound was coming toward us!

"Ahhhh! Madame! It's going to eat us!" I screamed.

Calmly, Madame said *tehillim* and we slowly repeated after

her word for word. When we finished, I dared to open my eyes. The creature was swimming closer and closer.

Madame opened a black box that she had brought along. She removed a fishing rod.

Despite my fear, I laughed. "Are you planning to catch that huge thing with that flimsy rod?"

"Oh, I think it'll be plenty," she answered.

She rowed closer to the floating grey mountain. Shuly and I closed our eyes. If we were going to be eaten by the creature, whatever it was, we didn't want to witness it.

Whack! Whack!

Was the monster eating us yet?

I opened my eyes a crack. Madame was standing in the boat, her hands clutching the fishing rod; she was whacking and smacking the sea creature!

My eyes opened wider, when I realized that every time she slammed the rod on the mound, the mound deflated and then blew up again.

Weird. Didn't look like a thrashing shark or whale to me.

I leaned over and then giggled. Shuly joined me when she realized what exactly we were looking at. It was no sea monster.

Madame finally hooked the "thing" and we held tightly on to the rod as she rowed back to shore, the huge mountain swimming behind us.

We saw people waving at us from the rocks. It looked as if the whole city had come to see Madame go fishing.

We hopped out of the boat and helped Madame schlep the creature out of the water. But it surely was no creature; it was a huge piece of discarded wood covered with a grey tarp that rose and fell with the waves.

The people cheered when they saw the "monster" all deflated and limp on the rocks. Madame quickly grabbed our hands and we made our way back home before anyone could question her.

However, we needed to ask. "Madame, how did you know that it wasn't a scary creature out there?"

She laughed. "*Mes petites*, Hashem made this world, and in a small lake which is surrounded on all sides by trees and rocks, no huge creature can suddenly appear. *Vraiment*, did you believe that it was some sort of monster?"

Uh…yeah…but I wasn't going to admit that to anyone.

So ended our sea creature saga. Everyone wanted to meet the brave pink woman who had saved the city, but by the time they finally traced her to our home, she was long gone back to France.

Fun with FOREIGN WORDS

monstre marin	Sea monster
on est prêts	We're ready
tu raconte des bêtes	You're telling me silly stories

DO YOU REMEMBER THESE?

alors	So
bien	Good
chèrie	Dear
mes petites	My little ones
non	No
vraiment	Really

The Feather of the Golden Eagle

Noooo!"

Shuly jumped away from the front lawn, while I stood staring at the falling glass and rolling beads. "Oh boy."

"This is not funny. What in the world will I do now?"

Shuly's eyes were round and big. "I think you should pretend that you didn't do it."

I backed away from the grass. "You think it'll work?"

"I don't know, but you know that I'm petrified of Chief Red Horse. I'm not going with you if you choose to apologize," she whispered.

Shuly raced up the stairs to our home. I stood outside and

saw the mess that I had made of the chief's door decoration. He was a Native American and a chief too. He was also a fierce, scary man. I certainly was not going to apologize by myself. He would probably swallow me whole and spit out my bones. Nope, I'd be safer at home. Under my covers. I ran in after Shuly and locked the door behind me. I took a deep breath and felt my heart beating crazy fast.

I was still panting when I came into the kitchen. Madame Chamberlaine was sitting at the table chatting with my mother. A fresh batch of vanilla buns was cooling on the counter. I sniffed my way over to the tray.

"Help yourself, *chèrie*." Madame smiled. Then she looked at me and in a second her hand was feeling my forehead.

"*Ma pauvre!* What happened? *Ça va?*"

The whole story came out. We were playing ball, Shuly and I, and we were of course seeing who could throw the ball stronger and farther. Guess who won? But while I did win, I also smashed Chief Red Horse's stunning glass decoration that was hanging on his front door.

Madame clucked her tongue. My mother stroked my hair when she said, "You know, you'll have to apologize."

"No way. I can't. He's too scary."

"She can't, Ma!" Shuly pleaded. "He's…he's…"

"He's what?" my mother asked.

"Tough and scary," I said. "I'm not going. No way no how."

"I'll come with you," Madame said.

I shook my head. "I'm still not going."

Madame looked at my mother and my mother looked at Madame. My mother shrugged. "You need to apologize, preferably before he notices the damage you did."

"Ma, you can't make me go. Please!"

"I won't force you to do anything. But it's the right thing to do. And it will be a *kiddush Hashem* if you own up to your mistake and apologize."

"I'll put money from my bank into his mailbox and I'll write him a note to say I'm sorry."

My mother pulled her lips tight. "That's like a second-best option."

I mumbled that I needed to do my homework and went to my room.

I couldn't concentrate. In any minute the chief would notice the broken glass and missing beads. He would be livid. He'd certainly guess that it was one of us who did it…and then what? Would I still hide and pretend it wasn't me? Would I let my mother apologize for me? I took a deep breath… Whoa, I was being the biggest sissy ever!

I made a mistake. But didn't my mother always say that the three most important words in the English language were "I am sorry"?

I straightened my back and blew the fright out of my heart. Even if the chief would bite me, I still needed to do the right thing.

I went back to the kitchen. My mother was cooking supper while Madame was packing up the buns.

"Will you come with me to apologize, Madame?"

Madame Chamberlaine hugged me tight. "*Ma petite, je le savais.* You brave, brave girl."

I felt ten feet tall when she said that. Was I being brave? I thought so. But I was doing something right too.

She took my hand and led me out the door. We crossed our

lawn and walked up the pathway to Chief Red Horse's brick house. The colorful beads had stopped rolling and the glass crunched beneath our feet.

My heart began to race again.

Madame rang the bell.

The door opened right away and there he stood, tall, broad, and very, very scary. His face was dark and full of grooves and wrinkles. His hands were extra-large and black around the nails.

"YES?" he bellowed.

I hid behind Madame's wide skirt. She gently pushed me forward.

Just then, the chief noticed the glass.

"WHAT IS THIS? WHO BROKE MY ORNAMENT?"

I hid again and nearly ran back home. But then I remembered that I was coming to apologize and Madame had called me brave. I am brave, I told myself. Watch me.

I swallowed and stepped forward. "Chief Red Horse, I am so, so sorry for breaking your decoration. It was a mistake and I promise to be more careful next time. Here." I thrust some dollar bills and coins in his direction. "This should be enough to buy you a new one."

"HA, HA, HA!" the chief laughed.

Was this supposed to be funny?

"LITTLE GIRL, YOU CAN KEEP YOUR MONEY. YOU ARE BRAVE TO OFFER AN APOLOGY. BRAVE LIKE ME! WAIT. I WILL SHOW YOU SOMETHING."

He disappeared into his house and came back with a tall headpiece that was full of beautiful, colorful feathers. He put it on his head.

"DO YOU KNOW WHAT THIS IS?"

I shook my head. I had seen such a thing in pictures, but I'd never seen anyone wearing one.

"THIS IS THE WITNESS TO MY BRAVERY."

(He sure wasn't too modest, but I wasn't going to tell *him* that.)

"EVERY TIME US NATIVES DO ANYTHING BRAVE, WE EARN ANOTHER FEATHER. THEN, WE PUT THEM ALL TOGETHER AND WEAR THEM ON OUR HEADS."

I nodded.

"DO YOU KNOW WHICH FEATHER WE GET FOR BEING VERY, VERY BRAVE?"

I shook my head.

"THIS ONE."

He showed me a beigey feather in his headpiece.

"IT IS A FEATHER FROM THE GOLDEN EAGLE!"

I nodded again. He must have done something incredibly brave to receive that feather.

"WAIT," he said as he went inside his home again.

He came back out holding a long, thin box.

"I HAVE BEEN WAITING TO GIVE SOMEONE THIS."

He carefully slipped off the cover. Inside was a feather.

I looked at the chief's headpiece. The feather was the same color as the feather of the golden eagle.

He smiled. "YOU ARE BRAVE. YOU CAME TO APOLOGIZE. YOU EARNED THE FEATHER OF THE GOLDEN EAGLE."

I was so shocked that I didn't know what to say.

"Thank you, Chief Red Horse."

Madame smiled. She too handed the chief a box.

"WHAT IS THIS?"

"For your kindness and understanding," she said.

The chief opened the cover. He sniffed.

"MMM! THIS I WILL EAT. THANK YOU."

We said good-bye and went back home, me with the feather of the golden eagle and Madame still clutching my trembling fingers.

Fun with FOREIGN WORDS

ça va	Are you okay
je le savais	I knew it
DO YOU REMEMBER THESE?	
chèrie	Dear
ma petite	My little one
ma pauvre	My poor

Stuck at the Beach

S o where are we going?" I asked Madame.

Shuly was looking out the window of the taxi, her nose pressed tight against the pane.

"Ah, *ma petite.* You'll smell it in a second."

"Are we going to the bakery?" I asked.

"*Oh là là! Bien, non.* Why would we go to the bakery when the cakes we prepare at home are so much fresher?"

I shrugged. "Well, what else can we smell before we arrive?"

"Wait, wait," Shuly yelled. "I smell it!"

I sniffed. "Huh?"

Shuly took a deep breath. "Ahh…the beach!"

"*Oui, chèrie,*" Madame said. "We are almost at *la plage.*"

"Shuly, did you hear that? *Plage*! Sounds like we'll be plunging into the water."

"I sure will."

We raced out of the taxi and into the hot sun. We removed our shoes when we got to the sand. Wow—so much sand! The tiny grains settled in my socks and rubbed between my toes. It was so amazing!

"I brought my *chaise* and my *parasol* so I can watch you, *mes filles*, run around while I will sit in comfort." She opened her *chaise* and positioned the *parasol* over her head.

What an afternoon. We made sand castles and sand cities, and we ate sandwiches that, for some reason, tasted quite sandy.

Finally, after my nose was starting to burn from the strong sun, Madame decided that we should start heading home. We packed up our beach gear. Madame closed her *parasol* and her *chaise* and we trudged up the sand to the road.

Madame held her long arm out to hail a taxi. One slowed down and the window rolled down.

"Where to?"

"We need to get home," Madame said as she opened the door.

"Hey," the cab driver yelled. "Are you coming from the beach?"

"*Oui, oui*, sir, and what a delight it was."

"Oh no. You can't come into my car! Do I look like a children's park to you? Do you think I like cleaning the sand from the seats?"

He drove off, his door still open.

Madame's eyes were bright and her usual pink cheeks were dark like cherries.

"*Oh là là*. Let's try another one."

She held out two fingers. Another cab slowed down.

The driver peered at all our stuff and shook his head. "Sorry, I have a policy not to take people back from the beach."

"But why not?" I asked.

"Look. Last five times I took passengers back from the beach, my car had so much sand in it that my son didn't want to go to the park anymore. He just wanted to play in the sand-box in my car."

And he was off.

"This is not fun," I said. "Madame, do you think we'll sleep on the beach tonight?"

She clucked her tongue. "*Ma petite*, Hashem will help."

The next taxi also refused to take us home. And so did the next, and the one after that, and so on. I could see that Madame's arm was getting tired of standing tall for so long.

Shuly began to cry. "I wanna go home! I wanna go home!"

We were tired and still wet from the water, and we were so, so full of sand. It sat like ants all over, scratching and bothering us. We just wanted to take a warm shower and go to sleep. But there we were, stuck on a highway with no way to get home because no driver wanted sand in his car!

The sun was winking to us and we could see that it too was getting ready to go to bed.

"Madame," Shuly sobbed. "It's getting dark. I'm scared."

Madame bent low to give us a sandy hug. I hate to admit it, but I began to cry too. (And wow, those tears tasted sandy!)

"Do not worry," she said. "We'll be home before you know it." She called a car service, but no one wanted to come out so far to get us. She tried flagging down some more cabs, but no one wanted to take us home.

By now Shuly was sitting on the side of the road, bawling out loud. I stood next to her and didn't cry, just my eyes were kind of wet because I was scared that we'd have to sleep on the beach, or maybe walk home, which would take us a couple of days.

"Call my parents," Shuly cried. "Maybe they can come and get us."

"*Chèrie*, your parents are at a wedding three hours from here, remember? There's no way they can come."

Madame came next to us and put her arms around our shoulders. "*Pauvre petites filles. Viens*, we will calm down and then we will have a blast."

We both looked at her. A blast? While we were stuck on this cold, lonely road?

"Madame," I said. "We're full of sand. How can we have fun with all these grains sitting in our clothes?"

She laughed. "Aha! You'll soon see."

She moved away from us a little bit and made a phone call. She spoke in French gibberish so we didn't understand what she said. When she came back, her pink tassels were swinging and she was smiling.

"We wait a little bit and then we are off."

"How?" I asked. "Did a taxi agree to take us?"

"You'll soon see."

She gave us some potato chips to eat, which tasted sandy, of course. But we ate and drank some sandy water and then waited some more.

"Madame," I said. "We're still stuck here and we're not having any fun yet."

"You will—ooh! I see him coming. Grab your bags and get ready to jump."

Shuly and I looked at the cars whizzing past. Which car was taking us home?

A huge dump truck stopped next to us. The motor was so loud that it looked like the truck was trembling. And what, you ask, was in the back of the vehicle?

Sand, sand, and more sand! Piles and piles and a mountain of it!

Shuly and I just stared.

"Madame Chamberlaine," I finally said. "Don't we have enough sand in our bags and clothes? Do we need another whole truck of it?"

Just then the passenger door opened and a man poked his head out. "Tante! So good to see you again!"

Madame helped us jump into the truck. The seats were wide and there was plenty of room for our bags.

Shuly's eyes were dry and so were mine. (But I wasn't really crying, remember? I certainly wasn't scared.)

"This is better than the beach!" I said as the truck rumbled down the highway.

Madame ruffled my sandy hair. "I told you Hashem would help. And I don't think Avi minds that we have sand in our clothes and bags, do you, Avi?"

We all laughed. It was a sandy ride home, but *oh là là* was it fun!

Fun with FOREIGN WORDS

chaise	Chair
la plage	The beach
parasol	Umbrella
petites filles	Little girls
sable	Sand
tante	Aunt

DO YOU REMEMBER THESE?

bien non	Why no
chèrie	Dear
ma petite	My little one
mes filles	My girls
oui	Yes
pauvre	Poor
viens	Come

Bubby Dvoshe

ubby Dvoshe?"

My mother smiled and nodded. "Yup, Bubby Dvoshe. Well, she's not really our grandmother, but she's related to us."

"When is she coming?" I asked.

My mother checked her watch. "Madame Chamberlaine said they'd be arriving just about now." She looked out the large window toward the street. "I'm a little worried. You see, Bubby Dvoshe is very, very old and she never traveled in an airplane before. In fact, I think she never traveled anywhere."

"Really?"

"Well, she lives in a village in Hungary where there's barely any electricity. I'm not sure how often she rides in a car."

Shuly and I looked at each other. "Huh? So how does she get to the store and stuff?"

My mother laughed. "You're going to like this. They travel in a horse and buggy."

"No way!"

She nodded. "Fun, no?"

We saw a taxi pulling up. We flew out the door when we saw the pink frills through the car window. Madame!

"Bonjour, *mes petites*," she called gaily as she stepped out in her pink heels.

We peeked into the taxi.

"Uh-oh," I said quietly. Shuly stared. Inside the car was the oldest, most shriveled-looking woman we had ever seen. She wore a colored scarf tied under her sagging chin and a green coat that looked like it must have been made when this woman was born.

"Wow," Shuly whispered. "She *is* old."

Madame practically had to carry her out of the taxi. Going up the steps was a bit complicated, but we made it and then settled Bubby Dvoshe on the couch with a tea. She looked at Madame Chamberlaine and smiled, her mouth full of gold teeth.

"You're very *csinos, köszönöm*." Her voice was scratchy and deep. "I...go...to...sleep," she said when she finished slurping her tea. "*Jó éjszakát*."

We all kept quiet as she shuffled into her room. We then heard snores coming from that direction.

"Good, she's asleep," Madame said. "Poor woman. This life must be a shock for her. She lives in one of those backward villages where there is some electricity, so lights they have, but they wash their clothes in the river and they live like they did almost a hundred years ago." She shook her head. "She was so miserable on the airplane. She held on to her armrests the entire flight. And when there was turbulence, *oh là là*. She was so frightened."

My mother looked sad. "It must be hard for her."

At four o'clock the next morning, I heard strange noises. I crept to my bedroom door and saw shadows in the bathroom. Think a robber would be interested in the bathroom? Nah. I went to look.

Standing over the bathtub was Bubby Dvoshe, her back rounded and the faucet going full force. I inched closer. Were those clothes she was scrubbing?

I turned my head to see Madame Chamberlaine joining me. "Good morning, *ma petite*." She peeked into the bathtub. "Bubby Dvoshe, you don't need to wash your clothes by hand. There is a washing machine in this house."

"Ah, but it can't wash my clothes as well as I can."

Madame laughed. "Oh yes. It does it better and makes you not work so hard. Come, I'll show you." She took Bubby Dvoshe's arm and I carried the bucket of wet clothes to the laundry room. Madame threw the stuff into the washing machine.

"*Voilà!*"

Bubby Dvoshe smiled. "I will wait here until it is finished."

I went back to my room to get dressed. Then I went to find Bubby Dvoshe. She was still in the laundry room, hanging her wet things over every available surface—on the door of the washing machine, on the laundry basket, over the top of the door.

"Bubby Dvoshe," I said. "We have a dryer."

"*Mit mondtál?*"

Oh no! French I spoke a bit, but Hungarian? *Oh là là!* I ran to get Madame.

Madame helped Bubby Dvoshe put her things in the dryer. When the load was finished, Bubby Dvoshe kept feeling the clothes as though she didn't quite believe that they could get dry by themselves.

When we were eating breakfast, I noticed how Bubby Dvoshe kept looking at the toaster, the coffeemaker, the hot water urn, the microwave.

So sad that she can't enjoy all the luxuries that we have, I thought. *She has to cook water on her stove and do everything from scratch. She's so old that she couldn't get used to this if she wanted to.*

"Oh, by the way," my mother said as Shuly and I left for school that morning. "I won't be home when you come back this afternoon. I think Madame Chamberlaine won't be here either. Bubby Dvoshe will be, though. Make sure she's comfortable, 'kay?"

"Sure!"

We ran to catch the bus.

Shuly and I came home at four o'clock. We unlocked the door expecting to find Bubby Dvoshe on the couch, but instead...a rush of noise hit us!

We ran into the kitchen. The noise was tremendous. Shuly and I just gaped. The kitchen was in shambles. The food processor was working on high, tiny chunks of carrot flying through the air like confetti. The coffeemaker was on, black liquid frothing out from every crack. The light of the microwave was on—which meant that it was turned on—and come to think of it, so were the lights of both the milchig and fleishig ovens! The kitchen smelled like something was burning. I ran to the ovens; both were on self-clean—the highest temperature they could be on! Every single appliance we owned was plugged in and powered on. We ran from one thing to the next, shutting them off.

When the kitchen was quiet, Shuly and I looked at each other.

"Uh-oh."

We both ran to the laundry room when we heard it. We burst out laughing. There were bubbles everywhere—on the floor, on the machines, and floating in the air. The washing machine was spitting out bubbles as it made the strangest noises. It looked like somebody overloaded the detergent compartment.

And, oh yeah, the dryer was on too.

"I think there was an electricity storm in our house," Shuly said. "Who in the world could have done all this?"

"Bubby Dvoshe?" I asked, because she was supposed to be the only one home.

"Impossible. She doesn't know the first thing about electricity, remember? She knows old-fashioned, and that's it."

"You think? Let's go find out."

There was noise coming from Bubby Dvoshe's bedroom too. The door was open a crack. Of course, we peeked in… and gasped.

Okay, folks, this was too funny and I've got to share what I saw. The treadmill was on, and old, wrinkled Bubby Dvoshe was sweating her kishkes out on it!

She smiled when she saw us, her gold teeth shining and

her kerchief slipping over her eyes. "*Allo!* This is fun. I...love... this!"

We laughed so hard that when Madame Chamberlaine came in, she couldn't get a word out of us. She looked into the room and Bubby Dvoshe was still power walking on the treadmill, though she was holding on to the bars for dear life.

Madame laughed until she had tears streaming down her cheeks. "And we thought she was old and outdated!"

When Bubby Dvoshe finally came off the treadmill, we sat her down and prepared her a cup of tea.

"Ah, life is exciting here, but you know, maybe life in Hungary is a bit calmer. And quieter."

Fun with FOREIGN WORDS

LET'S UNDERSTAND THE HUNGARIAN TOO. READY?

csinos	Cute, nice looking
köszönöm	Thank you
jó éjszakát	Good night
mit mondtál	What did you say

DO YOU REMEMBER THESE?

ma petite/mes petites	My little one(s)
voilà	Here you go

The 3-D Project

Hmm…who can I use as my hero?" I asked Shuly.

"Hero for what?"

"Morah Jacobs gave us this huge assignment. I think she thinks we're bored because even if I work on this project for two weeks without sleeping, eating, or going to school, I still wouldn't finish."

"*Oh là là*, sounds like a tough one."

"Tough? Impossible. Listen to this: 'For this assignment, you need to choose a hero. A hero is someone you admire because he or she is brave or has very fine *middos*. Your hero must be a real, living person. Using modern technology, you will portray this hero of yours in a unique and interesting way.'"

Shuly groaned. "You're right. This is gonna take you until you're old and grey."

"Yeah, and by then I won't even remember what I'm supposed to write about."

"Hey, I know. You have a hero!"

"I do?"

"Duh! She's kind and happy and always makes everyone around her happy."

I couldn't think. "Who?"

"Oh, come on. Clue number one: She's French."

"Madame! What a great idea. She has fine *middos* and I certainly admire her. But how can I portray her using modern technology?"

Shuly thought. "Is an oven considered modern technology? She bakes these yummy pastries. Maybe you can bring some in to your teacher. She'll give you an A if you let her take some home."

"Yeah, but only if they taste as good as Madame's stuff."

"You're right. Hmm… Maybe you can take some of the pastries she left in our freezer to the new 3-D printshop they opened down the block. Maybe they can print you some more of the pastries."

I grabbed the box from the freezer. "Fantastic. I think teachers should start coming to you for ideas. Tell Ma where I went."

No luck at the store, though. The man informed me that although there were 3-D printers for food, he didn't have one yet.

"Can you at least print these boxes with the pretty pink ribbon?"

"Sure. How many do you need?"

"Ten."

"Come back in an hour. I'll have them ready."

As I was walking home, a crazy thought went through my head. If the man could print boxes, maybe he could print Madame Chamberlaine! 3-D was as modern as technology could get.

I ran back to the store. I opened my purse and took out a picture of Madame. "Can you print this too?"

"Sure."

I left the store thrilled. So I wasn't going to be all wrinkled and bent when I finished the project!

An hour later, I was back. The man handed me a box. "These are the boxes you wanted."

The box was light; that was good. He walked around the counter and stood next to a tremendous box taller than me and very, very wide.

"And this is yours too."

My eyes nearly jumped out of my head. "What's inside?"

The man furrowed his brow. "You mean you ordered something but you don't know what it is?"

Well...yeah, but I didn't say that to him.

"These are the ten printouts of the lady you wanted."

"Ten?"

The man looked at me as if I had suddenly sprouted horns. "You okay?"

I began to cry. I had been so excited that I was almost done and he printed me ten Madame Chamberlaines? How would I pay for that and how in the world would I take them home?

The man felt bad. He called someone from the back.

A woman came out. "Hi, I'm Rikki. I'm Yankel's wife. What's the matter?"

She listened as I sobbed my problem to her. "Fine, it was a mistake. You ordered ten copies of the boxes so my husband assumed you wanted ten copies of the woman too. But we won't charge you for the extra nine. And tell you what. If you can get this Madame to fill up one box with her pastries and bring them over here, we'll deliver this huge box to your school."

"Will you? Wow, you're the best." I told them that I needed the big box for Thursday and schlepped the smaller box home.

I came to school early on Thursday to set up my project. As promised, the box was there. I tipped it over and found ten lifelike versions of Madame Chamberlaine inside. I set them up around the classroom and put a box in each set of hands.

I smelled something. Quite a good smell, actually. I opened one box and gasped. I had left the boxes empty, but this one was filled with tiny sweet-smelling pastries! I opened another box—also full! All of the boxes were full of tiny cinnamon, chocolate, and divine vanilla cakes! I then remembered that the box had felt heavier that morning. One minute—who did this? No one could bake pastries like Madame.

I looked around expecting her to walk through the door, but all was quiet. It was a little creepy. I finished setting up quickly and went outside to wait for my classmates. My friends walked in and were shocked by all the 3-D printouts of Madame.

"Who is that?"

"My hero."

"And what is that yummy smell coming out of the boxes she's holding?"

"You'll soon find out."

Morah Jacobs came in and smiled when she saw the real-looking Madames standing guard throughout her classroom.

*/, */, */,

"This is my hero," I began after davening. "She is so kind, so helpful, and always makes me smile. She always wears the color pink and bakes delicious pastries. She speaks French and I wish I could show you how she laughs."

There came a delightful sound from the corner of the room.

It was a *lot* creepy.

Then I noticed one of the large printouts was moving. What, did 3-D make things move too?

The large, plastic Madame Chamberlaine was walking toward me.

"Ahhhh!"

"*Chèrie*, do not be afraid. I'm real. Feel me!"

"Madame, how you scared me," I said as I hugged her.

"Who do you think filled up the boxes?"

"Well, now I know it was you. But how did you know to come?"

Madame glanced at Morah Jacobs and winked. "My hero."

"Your hero, Madame?"

She smiled. "*Vraiment*, wouldn't you love to know who that is, eh?"

I nodded and so did all the girls in my class. But Madame just smiled and wouldn't say. Meanwhile, I should tell you that I got the highest mark on this project, and guess what? I'm still young and healthy with no grey hairs on my head!

DO YOU REMEMBER THESE?	
chèrie	Dear
vraiment	Really

All the Colors of the Rainbow

inch me, Shuly. I don't believe this is real."

Shuly giggled. "If I pinch you and you wake up, then I'll be in France all on my own."

"Ha. So maybe don't pinch me because this must be real and then I'll pinch you right back and we'll get into this major fight and then Madame Chamberlaine will not be *contente*."

We wheeled our suitcases out of the airport and looked around.

"She said she'd be waiting for us right here."

Then we saw her, tassels flying behind her as she ran in her pink high heels.

"*Mes petites! Oh là là*, I'm *contente* that you came. Finally!"

She hugged us and took both our suitcases, and led us to the parking lot.

"This is your car, Madame?"

"*Bien oui*. Do you like it?"

It was a little pink Beetle, with a bunch of pink daisies on the dashboard.

"Nice." We giggled as we piled in.

We should've guessed that Madame would have a car like that. What else would she drive—a pink school bus?

She drove us to her apartment. It was quiet and smelled amazing. She gave us both plates heaping with mouthwatering pastries.

"*Manges, chèries.*"

Boy, did we eat.

"When you are rested you will meet my children."

My eyes opened wide. "Madame, you have children?"

She laughed. "*Bien sûr*. Why not?"

I shrugged. "I dunno. I guess I always thought you belong to…us."

She smiled. "I do, *ma petite*. But I have wonderful children too."

"Big? Little?"

"Oh, all married. But wonderful just the same."

We rested and then Madame drove us to the Eiffel Tower.

"My children are waiting for you here. I must run to visit old Mrs. Fromper, so they will take care of you. I have shown them a picture of you so they will find you right away. Don't worry; they'll be watching you the whole time. *Au revoir!*"

And just like that, we were on our own in a huge city with

a huge tower next to us. Shuly and I looked at each other. This couldn't be real.

"Pinch me now, Shuly," I said. "I think I want to wake up this time."

We looked around rather fearfully. Tons of people, speaking many different languages, were walking around. We looked up. Wow, the Eiffel Tower was so, so tall.

We walked around the tower, which between you and me wasn't all that interesting. It was just a bunch of steel.

"What now?" I asked.

Shuly shrugged.

Suddenly, this huge dog came barreling toward us, barking. I stood in shock as it came right up to my waist and barked more, his disgusting saliva dribbling on my hands.

I was shaking. I was petrified. I wanted to run, but was too scared to do anything.

A woman appeared at my side. She shooed away the dog with harsh words and then put her arm around my trembling shoulders.

"*Ma petite*, are you okay?"

She sounded just like Madame Chamberlaine. I turned to look at her and my mouth opened in shock.

The woman looked like Madame too, but instead of wearing all pink, she wore a purple scarf, a purple skirt, purple high heels, and even her cheeks had a purple tinge.

"Madame Chamberlaine?" I asked.

She laughed. The same tinkling laugh as Madame.

"I'm her daughter Chedva. I've been watching you from this bench since my mother dropped you off. I waited for you to recognize me. So pleased to finally meet you!" She hugged Shuly and me.

"Thank you for saving me from that dog," I told her.

Chedva waved her hand. "Nonsense. Hashem put me here at the right time."

"Are you her only child?"

She laughed again. "*Non*. You'll soon meet the others."

She led us down a small path and stopped. We stopped too. And stared and stared. Then we laughed and laughed and laughed. Sitting on four benches was the funniest thing we'd ever seen.

There was a bunch of women all dressed alike. They each wore a scarf with tassels hanging at the bottom, a long, flowing skirt, and high heels. But the craziest thing was that none of them were wearing the same color. One woman was dressed all in green. Another all in blue. And there was turquoise, yellow, orange, black, brown, peach, gold, silver, ivory, lilac, lime, light blue, maroon, and fuchsia!

The women all smiled and waved. "*Bonjour!*"

"You are all Madame's children?"

They nodded.

"Wow! That's a whole lot. But how is it that you all look like her? Aren't any of you her daughters-in-law?"

They laughed.

"Madame Chamberlaine has no sons. We're an all-girl family."

"That must've been so much fun growing up. How many are you?"

"Seventeen."

"What? How in the world did Madame manage just...

driving you around, like to school and stuff?"

"Oh, you'll find out soon. Now come, we need to get something before our mother comes for us."

They all stood up.

"We should've thought to bring along a tasseled scarf and high heels," I whispered to Shuly. "I feel so out of place next to all of them."

Shuly giggled. "I would pick the color…hmm…maybe teal?"

"Teal is almost like turquoise and one of them is already dressed in that color. You'd have to choose something simpler, like white."

"Fine. And you could take grey. But since nobody told us about this *tichel* party, we'll have to stay in our regular clothes."

The women approached a beautiful garden. They each picked two flowers and then put all of them into a gigantic bunch. They paid the owner and went to the gate to wait.

"Why do you need so many flowers?" I asked.

Chedva said, "This is something we started when we were little. We wanted to show our mother how much we loved and appreciated her, so we would pick flowers for her and she would put them on the dashboard of her car. We still do it every week and she loves it."

"Do you mind if the two of us buy her some flowers too, to show our appreciation and love?" Shuly asked.

"*Bien sûr!* She would be delighted."

So we went back and bought four flowers, and added them to the bunch. We returned to the group of ladies just as a long pink bus painted with colorful flowers pulled up. They motioned us over and began piling inside.

"Is that how we're going home?" I wondered.

I went on the bus after everybody else. And, surprise! Madame Chamberlaine was sitting behind the wheel.

"You found my wonderful daughters, I see. I hope you had fun."

"*Bien sûr*, Madame. They're just as kind and as much fun as you are."

Madame dropped her daughters off and then we chugged back to her house.

"*Mes petites*," Madame said as she served us supper. "I see you are tired."

We giggled as we tried to hide more yawns.

"You will go to sleep and tomorrow we will go on a trip."

"Trip?" I stopped yawning and sat up. "Where to?"

Madame smiled. "Well, somewhere wet, but hopefully *you* will not get wet!"

"Wet, but not us?" Shuly and I looked at each other.

"Swimming pool, maybe?"

"Dodo, swimming usually gets you wet," Shuly answered.

"Hmm, maybe the beach?"

Shuly shrugged. She was too tired to think.

Madame smiled and shooed us out of the kitchen and into our bedroom.

"You will find out soon enough."

＼′⁄ ＼′⁄ ＼′⁄

We were just finishing breakfast when Madame Chamberlaine said, "So were you able to sleep even though you were so curious about our trip?"

Shuly and I laughed. "We were so tired that we didn't even have time to think. But do tell us!"

"We're going to see the Seine."

"Seine? What's that?" I asked. "You mean the sun?"

Madame laughed. "I most certainly do not mean the sun. We're going to see the Seine River."

"Ooh! I'm ready."

"I have to make sure my girls can come with us. Let me call them."

I turned to Shuly. "This is going to be fun if all seventeen of them can come along."

Madame was jabbering in French on the phone. Then she clapped her hands. "All settled then. We'll leave in *cinq minutes*."

I stared at Madame. "You spoke to all seventeen of them in under a minute and all of them agreed to be ready in five minutes. Don't they have jobs and kids?"

She smiled. "Well, Tuesday morning is our usual get-together time. Today we'll take you on a cruise on a *bateau mouche* on the Seine River."

We went out and Madame led us to her pink bus. The flowers from the day before still lay on the dashboard. They were a bit droopy, but still looked colorful and alive.

Madame stopped every few streets to pick up another daughter. They came onto the bus with smiles.

"*Bonjour! Commen ça va?*"

We smiled back and nodded. "*Bien, bien.*"

We got to the river and piled out of the bus and into the *bateau mouche*. The river was calm and peaceful and the boat pulled out.

Chedva started a game of broken telephone and we all giggled and whispered into each other's ears. Shuly and I didn't understand what we were being told because the ladies were talking to us in French. I mean, I have picked up some French words, but when someone talks all in French to me, it sounds like one long *rrrr* with water stuck in the throat!

Soon, we grew tired and went to stand by the railing on the deck. We watched the ripples in the river and how the sun made the water look like it was dancing and shimmering.

A woman I didn't recognize stood next to me. She held a cute baby in her arms. I smiled at him, and he reached over and gave my hair a good yank. He kept pulling. People were all around me and I was being pushed from both sides. I tried to keep my head away from the little one, but he kept reaching for my hair again and again—he was strong! It hurt when he pulled. The mother didn't seem to notice, so I said, "*Bébé. Cheveux.*"

The woman nodded her head. "*Oui, oui. C'est jolie, eh?*"

Chedva, who was also standing beside me, quickly explained to the woman what was going on. The woman felt terrible. She turned to apologize but as she did, of course the baby stretched his pudgy hand and yanked my hair again. Ouch and double ouch!

The lady turned red from embarrassment. But the baby saw that his mother was not paying too much attention to him and he jumped. He went right through the gate that surrounded the rim of the boat!

We all stared. The baby was over the gate and on the edge of the boat! Another second and he'd be in the river. The poor mother was in shock.

I was the closest to the baby, so I stuck my hand through the railing to reach him. But, oh no, he wiggled.

I reached further out and stuck my whole body through the gate to get him. One of his toes was extending past the ledge. I grabbed him. Everyone behind me started breathing again and clapping.

"*Oh! Merci! Merci!*" the mother shouted, tears running down her cheeks.

I handed her the baby. As she grabbed him, she accidentally pushed my hand and...*splash*! I tumbled right into the freezing water.

"Help!" I yelled as the water filled my nose and then my mouth.

I saw Madame waving to me.

"Help me, Madame!" I shouted. She was trying to untangle a life preserver. Obviously, it wasn't working. "Quick! I'm... gon...na...drown!"

Between the splashes of icy water, I saw lots of people coming to help her. It looked like the rope was stuck and they couldn't throw the life preserver to me. I felt the water pulling me down. I waved my hands.

"Help! Help!"

Then I saw something fly over the white railing, and there was Madame treading the water right next to me!

"Madame," I said as water filled my mouth.

She swam close to me and put her arms around my chest. She pulled me to the other side of the boat, where someone was throwing a different life preserver into the water. Madame grabbed the floating white ring.

"Here, hold tight," she said.

"But what about you?" I asked.

"I'll go after you. I'm a good swimmer."

"No, come with me," I begged.

"Go, *chérie*. I'll be up in a jiffy."

Two burly men pulled the rope. I fell into Chedva's arms when I felt the wooden floor beneath my feet. I watched as they lowered the rope once more for Madame.

But she wasn't there anymore!

"Hey, where is she?" someone yelled.

Everyone started screaming at once. Madame's colorful daughters quickly gathered together next to the railing and started saying *tehillim*. Chedva kept her arm around my shivering shoulders. I began to cry. All because she wanted to save me! Maybe she drowned, maybe she was hurt. Oh, this was way too scary…and then, there she was!

She was stepping over the gate and sat down beside me. She calmly squeezed the dripping water out of the hem of her skirt. And she was still wearing her pink high heels.

My eyes opened in shock. "Madame Chamberlaine! How… how in the world did you get here?"

"Shh, doesn't matter. I'm here. Are you all right?" She wrapped a dry towel around my shoulders.

"Yeah, but…how?"

Chedva laughed. "My mother's not a magician. She probably found a ladder or rope at the side of the boat."

Madame smiled, her eyes twinkling in the sunlight. She wagged a finger. "Chedva, you know me too well!"

Well, the boat turned around and let us all off. We'd had more than enough for one day. Madame took home her girls and then we relaxed on her couch with warm chocolate milk and delicious pastries.

"So, *mes petites*, what shall we do tomorrow?"

We were too tired to think.

"How about we visit the old age home? I usually go there on Wednesdays and you can help me schlep all the pastries and things I usually bring to them.

"Madame, anything with you is fun. We can just be home and we'll still have fun."

"Glad you think so, *chèries*. But it's even more fun when we help others have fun too. So it's to the home tomorrow. Be up bright and early!"

\\'/ \\'/ \\'/

We were up bright and early all right. We schlepped boxes and boxes of pastries and drinks to the old age home. We sang to the elderly people, spoke to them, held their hands, and they ours. Time passed fast; when we looked at our watches we realized that it was already late afternoon!

"Wow, Madame. That was wonderful, but I think I hear my stomach growling," I said.

"You think?" Shuly said. "Well, I know that my stomach is growling. I can eat a whole box of pastries."

"Yeah, me too!"

Madame led us to her bus. We went on and watched her rummage under the seats.

She straightened up and held two boxes in her hands.

"Young ladies, you certainly deserve this. One box of pastries for you and one for you," she said, handing each of us a box.

"No way."

"Madame, how did you know to bring this along?"

She smiled. "I guess you can say that I know my little friends."

I made a *berachah* and bit into a cake. Yum.

"Are you really tired or are the two of you up for some more fun?"

"Madame, aren't you tired?"

She laughed. "Not with the two of you around. You helped me so much today that my work took half the time. So do you want to go on a picnic or not?"

"Is that even a question? Oh yes!"

"My daughters are waiting for us in a park. Lots of fun equipment there that you can play with. Let's go."

We had a marvelous time chatting and playing, but we couldn't eat. Shuly and I both polished off a half a box of pastries before we got there. If we would've put one more thing in our stomachs...*oh là là*!

It started getting dark and we climbed into the pink school bus. Madame revved the motor.

I fell into the worn pink seat next to Shuly. "Whew. It's been a crazy day."

"Yeah," Shuly said. "It's been busy and fun." She closed her eyes. "I'm exhausted. Can you believe we're going home tonight?"

"Too bad. It's been awesome getting to know Madame Chamberlaine's family. Her daughters are nearly as much fun as she is."

Chedva popped her head over the back of the seat behind us. "Only 'nearly' as much fun?" she asked with a twinkle in her eye.

We laughed. "Well, even 'nearly' is a lot more fun than most people!"

"Here, look," she said. "We brought you a little gift to remember us."

She handed us a wrapped box. Shuly ripped the glittery paper off and opened it.

"Wow, it's the cutest thing."

They gave us a miniature pink school bus. It even had colorful flowers on the dashboard!

"*Merci! Merci!*" we said to all the ladies.

They all smiled and chatted to us—in French, of course. Don't tell them, but most of the time we just nodded and pretended that we understood what they were saying. Really, we didn't have a clue! They usually didn't notice unless they asked us a question, and we just kept nodding... but then they stood there waiting for an answer. A liiittle embarrassing, but we couldn't learn a whole language in a few days, especially when these ladies tended to speak a mile a minute!

We heard a loud, grating noise and the bus stopped.

"*Oh là là,*" Madame said.

Her daughters groaned and dropped their faces into their hands.

"*Pas encore!*"

Shuly and I looked from woman to woman. What was going on?

We heard honking and yelling coming from behind us.

"*Viens, mes filles,*" Madame said as she stood up from her seat and opened the door. Her daughters all piled off the bus.

I looked at Shuly. She looked at me. What in the world was happening?

We quickly got off the bus too. Then we stared.

Madame Chamberlaine and all her daughters were standing behind the bus, their shoulders against the frame, and they were pushing with all their might. Chedva jumped away and leaped into the driver's seat. The women continued pushing; their faces became red and sweaty.

Shuly and I burst out laughing. It was the funniest sight we had ever seen. Madame, dressed in pink, and her daughters, looking exactly like her but dressed in different colors, were pushing a bus?

Well, seemed like we weren't the only ones who thought it was funny because all the cars passed stopped to honk, wave, and smile.

"Why aren't we helping them?" Shuly asked.

"Of course!"

We ran to push too, and before we knew it the bus got to the side of the road.

"Now what?" I asked as the women took a minute to wipe their foreheads.

Chedva came out of the bus. "This happens all the time. This bus is older than our great-great-grandmother. When we were young and my mother used to take us to school, and this happened...*oh là là*! We were so embarrassed to push the bus in the middle of the street. But we've done it so many times that we don't care anymore."

"But what happens now?" I asked. "How do you make it work again?"

"Oh, my mother has taken it to the garage so many times

that they've gotten tired of seeing her. They told her to either dump the bus or learn to fix it on her own."

Shuly giggled. "I guess she learned to fix it on her own."

Chedva nodded. "She sure did. There she goes right now."

There she went indeed. Madame disappeared under the pink bus! All we could see were her pink heels sticking out.

We heard tinkering and banging, then Madame stuck her head with the pink-tasseled *tichel* out. "Chedva, can you come give me a hand down here?"

Chedva disappeared under the bus too. Then all we saw were two pairs of high heels sticking out from under the bus, one pink and one purple. Then we heard, "Gila! Golda! Baila! Rina! Maman needs your help here too!"

Gila in green, Golda in yellow, Baila in blue, and Rina in orange disappeared under the bus. Now it was funny seeing high heels of all those colors sticking out from under it!

"You think she needs our help too?" I asked Shuly.

"Doesn't hurt to ask."

But as we were bending down, Madame came out. She wiped her grimy hands on a towel. She wasn't smiling.

"*Maman, çe ne va pas?*"

She pressed her lips into a tight line. "*Non.*"

The ladies all groaned again.

Suddenly we heard a tremendous noise of a sputtering motor and honking. A van, the color of sand, which looked like it was probably the first van that was ever produced, stopped behind us.

A little old lady in a short grey sheitel, wearing huge red sunglasses, came running over to Madame. She pounced on her and wrapped her in a hug.

Madame stared at the woman at first, but then laughed. "Madame Sabbah! You look exactly like you did when you taught me."

Madame Chamberlaine turned to us. "This is my first grade teacher." Then she winked and whispered, "She must be over a hundred and twenty."

The old lady pointed a thin, long finger. "Not nice, Madame, to tell them how old I am. What's the problem with your bus?"

Madame told her that she was missing a part. It must have fallen on the road further back.

The old lady sprinted to her car. She came back with something in her hand. "You mean this?"

I'd never seen Madame Chamberlaine shocked, but right then she was. "Where did you find that?"

"Well, like you said, I'm not young; when I was growing up we never threw anything in the garbage like they do today. So as I was driving here, I saw this piece on the road. I drove right next to it, opened my car door, and grabbed it before anyone else could. Good thing I did, eh?"

Madame thanked her and slid under the car. A few minutes later, she was up and smiling.

"*Merci beaucoup, Madame Sabbah!*"

The old woman waved and skipped back to her van. She roared off.

We all climbed back into the bus and got home without any stops or breakdowns. We quickly prepared for our trip back. And you can well imagine that the miniature pink bus we received sits proudly on our dresser (and never gets stuck, by the way!).

Fun with FOREIGN WORDS

au revoir	See you
bateau mouche	Open-excursion boats
bébé	Baby
c'est jolie	It's pretty
çe ne va pas	It's not working
cheveux	Hair
cinq	Five
commen ça va	How are you
maman	Mommy
manges	Eat
pas encore	Not again

DO YOU REMEMBER THESE?

bien	Good
bien oui	Of course
bien sûr	Certainly
bonjour	Good day, hi, hello
chèrie(s)	Dear(s)
contente	Happy
merci	Thank you
merci beaucoup	Thank you very much
mes filles	My girls
ma petite/mes petites	My little one(s)
non	No
oui	Yes
viens	Come

Words to Know

You should be a French pro by now. (If you aren't yet, here's some help!)

alors: So

arrêtez: Stop

au revoir: See you

aujourd'hui: Today

autobus: Bus

avec: With

avec plaisir: With pleasure

bateau mouche: Open-excursion boats

bébé: Baby

bien: Good

bien non: Why, no

bien oui: Of course

bien sûr: Certainly

bon: Good

bon anniversaire: Happy birthday

bon nuit: Good night

bonjour: Good day, hi, hello

boucle d'oreilles: Earrings

c'est jolie: It's pretty

ça va: You okay

cartable: Schoolbag

çe ne va pas: It's not working

çela appartient a toi: Does this belong to you

chaise: Chair

chat: Cat

chaque minute: Every minute

chère, chèrie(s): Dear(s)

cheveux: Hair

chocolat chaud: Hot chocolate

cinq: Five

commen ça va: How are you

comprendez vous: Do you understand

contente: Happy

délicieux: Delicious

écoutez: Listen

et vous: And you

exactement: Exactly

fille(s): Girl(s)

goutez une: Taste one

je le savais: I knew it

je ne sais pas: I don't know

je suis contente: I am happy

la plage: The beach

maintenant: Now

mais: But

mais oui: Why, yes

maman: Mommy

manges: Eat

merci: Thank you

merci beaucoup: Thank you very much

merveilleux/merveilleuse: Marvelous

moi: Me

monstre marin: Sea monster

neige: Snow

non: No

on est prêts: We're ready

on va s'amuser maintenant: We will have some fun now

on y va: Let's go

oui: Yes

parasol: Umbrella

pas encore: Not again

pauvre: Poor

petite(s): Little one(s)

pour toi: For you

prête: Ready

quoi: What

s'il vous plait: Please

sable: Sand

tante: Aunt

toi aussi: You also

très bien: Very good

trois: Three

tu parle français: You speak French

tu raconte des bêtes: You're telling me silly stories

un petit peu: A little bit

une bonne et douce annèe: A happy and sweet year

viens: Come

vite: Fast

voilà: Here you go

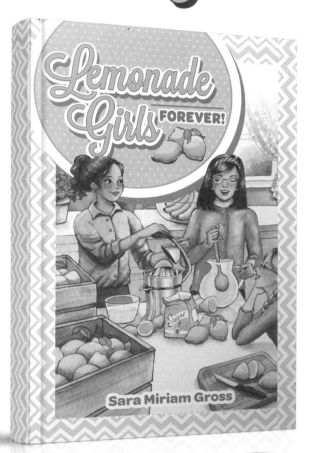

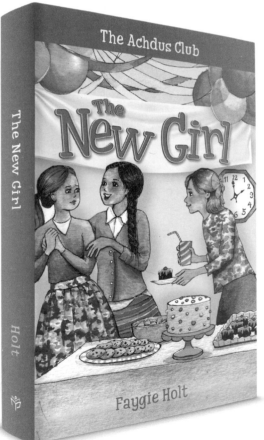